SW

D0508621

THE
...OTERION
MISSION

THE SOTERION MISSION

STEWART ROSS

Curious
Fox

First published in 2013 by Curious Fox, an imprint
of Capstone Global Library Limited,
7 Pilgrim Street, London, EC4V 6LB – Registered
company number: 6695582

www.curious-fox.com

First published in 2011 as a serialised ebook by
Fiction Express (www.fictionexpress.co.uk)

ISBN 978 1 782 02014 1
17 16 15 14
10 9 8 7 6 5 4 3

A CIP catalogue for this book is available from the
British Library.

Cover images:
Shutterstock – © Matthew Strauss; © robodread
istockphoto – © coloroftime

Typeset in Palatino 10pt

Printed and bound by CPI Group (UK) Ltd, Croydon, CR0 4YY

This book is gratefully dedicated to Eloise,
Laura, Lucy, Luke, Meg, Molly, Paul,
Seamus and the host of others who helped
guide the Mission.

Contents

The Long Dead
2106

Later, as his eyes became accustomed to the gloom, he noticed a sheet of paper lying on the desk. It was dry and crackled in his fingers when he brought it nearer the light. As he slowly deciphered the faded handwriting, his eyes widened in surprise. It was a letter, a message from the Long Dead.

Greetings –

I imagine you're reading this, whoever you are, because you want to know what this place is all about. I'll try and explain as briefly as I can – I haven't got much time left.

Back in May 2017, an epidemic of what we called the Mini-flu struck the world. Everyone got it but, as the slight symptoms lasted only a few hours, no one took much notice. They should have. The disease was mutating the mechanism in our DNA that controls ageing. The delayed effect kicked in from August 2018.

Before this we had aged slowly, many of us living to 70, 80 or even 100. Not any more. Nowadays everyone suddenly grows old and dies during their 19th year. The speed of change is terrifying – 3-4 weeks at most. We call it the "Death Month".

Adults over 19 went first, billions of them. Services collapsed, power failed, plagues swept the planet, rotting bodies piled in the streets. In a few short months, science, literature and knowledge – thousands of years of human civilization – disintegrated. Fortunately or not, we were saved from full-scale warfare because governments ordered the destruction of all domestic and military weaponry immediately they saw what was going on.

Less than a year has passed since it all began – and it's mayhem out there. Law and order have broken down and gangs of desperate teenagers terrorise the streets and countryside. I can understand how they feel. They know their 18th birthday is their last: at some point during the next 365 days they'll wake up to find their skin a little tighter and flecks of grey in their hair. They'll be in their Death Month, with just days to live. There are many suicides.

I'm one of the last old-style adults. As my Death Month started about three weeks ago, I reckon I've got only a few hours to go. By the end of July, there won't be a single one of us left.

I guess you understand something of what I'm talking about. Your DNA – if you understand what that is – must be the same as ours. That means you and the people you live with are all 18 or younger. I can't imagine your world, though it must somehow have evolved out of ours – the one you can probably see in ruins all about you.

So, what's this strange depository you've managed to get into? Racing against time, a group of us have tried to secure a tolerable future for our kids. We've set up camps for them to manage on their own when we're gone. Maybe you're from one of these? I hope so.

We've also built this place, a secure vault containing all the human knowledge and wisdom we could gather. It's for you, young stranger – as long as you're able to access it. We've included the data of the Salvation Project, a medical programme aimed at reversing the DNA-altering symptoms of the Mini-flu. The scientists died before their work was finished. I don't know how close they came to success.

I trust you'll be able to use what you find here. It may allow you to pick up the pieces and carry on where we left off. Try and make a better fist of it than we did! With that wish in mind, I've named this vault after an ancient word for salvation: Soterion, the only place of hope in a world looking so desolate that it breaks my dying heart.

Dr Rebekkah Askar
10 July 2019

1
A Refugee

As the first cold light of dawn fingered through the forest, she rose from the ground and ran. Silently at first, afraid of waking the guards, then recklessly, her dark hair streaming behind her like an ancient warrior of legend.

Thorns tore her flimsy clothing and clawed at her bare legs. Soon she was panting heavily, mouth open, gasping in the damp morning air. Still she ran, desperately and blindly towards the rising sun.

On the edge of a glade, she paused for breath. Dogs. Had they discovered her absence and unleashed the hounds? If they had, she was doomed. They would hunt her down like a beast and circle her, laughing as they watched their animals tear her to pieces. Worse, if they managed to pull the hounds off before she died, they would drag her back as a trophy for him.

To the Zeds, "mercy" was an obscenity.

Chest heaving, she raised her head and listened. Nothing. Just birdsong and the busy hum of early insects. No, wait. Far away, deep within the thickness of the forest, she heard the first unmistakable howl. They were on to her.

There was no hiding. Wherever she went, the keen noses of the hounds would seek her out. Her only option was to keep running. Terror gave her new strength, and before long the trees had thinned to a stony incline of tired scrub. Partly on all-fours like a wild animal, she scrambled to the top and looked down.

It was a dream that unfolded below her, a miracle. On the floor of a green valley watered by a wide river, a small community clustered around what remained of a Long Dead farmhouse. Beside it stood several stone buildings and a scattering of rough wooden huts. Smoke from a dozen fires curled lazily into the clear air. Nearer to her, reached by a wooden bridge, stretched broad fields protected by spiked barricades and watchtowers.

She gasped in amazement. They were Constants. Quite by chance, she had stumbled upon a community of her own kind. If she could get down the slope and cross the plain to the boundary, she would be among friends, safe.

The barking was louder now, and approaching fast. Spurred on by hope, bounding, sprinting, leaping, sometimes falling and rolling out of control, she careered down the side of the valley in a small avalanche of dust and stones. At the bottom, she glanced up to see the first pursuers silhouetted on the crest above. One of the dogs was already bounding down the slope towards her. To her left, an arrow fell harmlessly into the damp grass.

The spikes and towers of the palisade were plainly visible, perhaps only 800 paces away. But even that was too far – though a strong runner, she couldn't possibly match the speed of hounds with the scent of a kill in their nostrils. The mission had failed.

At that moment, a bell clanged within the distant community. Hearing it, a thousand bright memories danced in her mind and the hint of a smile momentarily lighted across a face already lined by fear and hardship. She rose to her feet, hope rekindled, and with pumping fists and straining legs, she ran again.

Cyrus was woken by the harsh clanging of the alarm. Attack! At first, he didn't believe it. The Zeds never made a move this early in the day, it was not their way. Emir Leiss said it was because they were too lazy or too stupid, or both. Cyrus closed his eyes again – the alarm went hammering on. It was for real.

Across the Constant community of Della Tallis, men and women who had seen more than eleven winters came stumbling out of the huts, wiping their eyes and blinking in the bright early morning light. All were armed, some with long bows, others with weapons fashioned from metal from objects made before the Great Death. Fully awake now, Cyrus stuffed a knife shaped from a car spring into his belt and grabbed the steel-tipped spear handed down to him from his grandfather. When no one lived to see nineteen winters, grandparents were remote, even legendary figures. Apparently his spear was a "niner" – its powerful thrusts had ended no less than nine Zed lives.

Cyrus hurried across the bridge and headed for his sector of the defence palisade. Navid, the same age but rounder in the face, stockier and bearing a long-handled axe with a blade that had once been a wheel, fell in alongside. Together they jogged into position to the right of the central watchtower. Corby,

Navid's huge, mud-coloured mongrel dog, lay on the grass beside them.

The two men peered over the pointed stakes towards where the valley floor rose steeply into the woods. Yes, it was an assault alright, but a strange one. It seemed to be headed by a single figure, with dogs and other runners following behind. Cyrus had fought off several Zed attacks since becoming a Defender six winters ago, but he had never before seen one that began like this. He glanced up at the watchtower from where Taja, the Mudir of the sector, gave her orders.

"What is it, Taja?" he called.

"I'm not sure. There are very few of them. Strange – the person out front looks like a woman. It's probably some sort of trick."

"Why the dogs?" Navid glanced down at Corby, whose ears were twitching at the sound of barking. "Thought they only used them for hunting?"

"They do." Taja paused, staring hard at the scene developing in front of her. "And it looks as if that's what they're doing here, hunting…that woman."

Her voice was level, matter-of-fact. A Mudir of eighteen winters, she was well known throughout the community for her intelligence and ability to stay calm under pressure.

As they watched, the leading figure began waving her arms and shouting. It sounded like a cry for help. Then, out of exhaustion or because the movement caused her to lose her balance, she tripped and fell forward.

The baying hounds, no more than fifty paces behind, closed

16

rapidly. Their quarry struggled to her feet and ran heavily on. Her screams were quite audible now.

"Help! Help me! Constant! Not Zed!"

Cyrus frowned. "She's one of us, Taja! We must shoot the dogs! For pity's sake, tell the archers to shoot the dogs!"

"I'm the Mudir, Cyrus, and I will make the decisions. I told you, it might be a trick."

Cyrus glanced again at the desperate woman. He was convinced that this was no act. The screams, the frantic gestures were too distressingly real. He hurried to the foot of the watchtower and looked up at the impassive Mudir.

"Please, Taja. For me."

Taja's face remained inscrutable. After a short pause she said quietly, "For you, Cyrus, yes. Just for you." Then she turned away, calling sharply, "Archers! Target the dogs, not the woman. Aim! Shoot!"

Two dozen arrows sped towards their target. Six of the eight hounds let out squeals of pain as the missiles sank deep into their taut flesh. Some died outright; the others, mortally wounded, lay panting and whimpering on the bloodstained grass. Seeing the carnage and not wishing to lose any more precious animals, their masters whistled for the two unharmed beasts to follow them and, shouting curses at the jeering Constants, retreated across the meadow into the forest.

Moments later, willing hands hauled the fugitive over the barricade and lowered her, quivering with fatigue and relief, to the ground. As Cyrus and Navid bent to help her, Corby began behaving strangely. Maybe it was the scent she brought with her, but he had been uneasy from the moment the good-looking stranger crossed the palisade. Growling quietly, he now went up to her and stood poised, like a guard, over the prostrate body.

"What's the matter, Corby?" asked Navid. "Something about her you don't like?"

The dog responded by sniffing at the woman's hair. Cyrus, who had cushioned her head on his knee so she could drink from the clay cup he held, pushed the creature away. "Don't be so daft, Corby!" he snapped, surprised by his own sharpness. "Get him off, Navid! He's being stupid."

"No, Cyrus," said a calm, confident voice above him. "The dog's quite right. It is we who have been stupid."

It was Taja. She had come down from the watchtower to interrogate the new arrival. With a slight frown, she knelt and swept back the long dark hair that had fallen across the woman's handsome face and brow. The onlookers gasped in dismay. Burned black and deep into the clear brown skin of her forehead was the unmistakable tattoo of a Zed.

"See!" barked Taja, springing back to her feet. "First appearances are deceptive, Cyrus. She's a Zed. Kill her!"

Had the Defenders been as certain as their Mudir, the outsider would have died there and then. But they knew Zeds were tattooed after five winters, and the mark on this woman, who looked as if she had seen at least seventeen, was still quite fresh and raw. Something was not quite right, and for a crucial moment no one moved.

"I repeat," said Taja, "kill her! Now!"

One of the Defenders slowly raised his heavy sword. Cyrus'

pulse quickened. Yes, the refugee carried the hated tattoo, he told himself, but it was not that simple. She was somehow different, almost special; no Zed was this dignified – and certainly not this attractive. Even if it meant questioning a Mudir's judgement, he had to do something.

But before he could speak, the woman herself lifted brilliant green eyes towards the sword poised over her and said quietly, "No, please don't! I am Roxanne, from the Constant community of Yonne. I was captured by the Zeds. They branded me with this tattoo to make me one of their own."

"Can you prove it?" demanded Taja, signalling to the executioner to lower his sword.

Roxanne pulled herself up until she rested on an elbow. "Yes, I will prove it, and I will explain everything."

She paused for a moment to drain the cup. "Thank you, Cyrus." Taking it back, he looked at her directly for the first time. The brilliance of her eyes unnerved him.

Turning quickly back to Taja, she went on, "And thank you for sparing my life. You see, before I was captured, I was on a mission, a mission to change the lives of all Constants for ever."

For a moment, Taja studied her curiously, carefully, like a cat trying to figure out the intentions of an intruder on its territory. Then, frowning slightly, she shifted her gaze towards Cyrus. Finally, she looked back at the refugee and nodded. Cyrus understood the gesture at once. It spoke of acceptance, not welcome, and granted Roxanne nothing more than a stay of execution.

On Taja's orders, Roxanne was escorted back to the farm. Here she was kept under close guard in the Prison Hut while Della Tallis' ruling council, the Majlis, assembled to hear her case.

The meeting was held in what had been the living room of the old farmhouse. The once-comfortable chamber was now little more than a barn. For generations nothing had been replaced or repaired. The glass in the windows was missing or broken, and the only items of furniture were rough wooden benches and a thick-legged pine table. A dirty shadow showed where a Long Dead ancestor had laid a carpet over the broken stone flags of the floor. Overhead, where once an electric light had shone, a bare, cobweb-strewn flex dangled from the cracked ceiling. Only the fireplace, broad and comforting, remained much as it had been in times past, an ash-strewn echo of former wonders.

For all its faded shabbiness, the chamber had a special significance for the settlement. It was a tangible link to the Long Dead. Though the rusting and crumbling constructions of those revered ancestors were gradually being repossessed by nature, the council room remained a practical symbol of a civilization the Tallins proudly strove to maintain. Its half-remembered principles and customs, like reaching council decisions by handshow, were what distinguished them from the despicable barbarity of the Zeds.

The Majlis was presided over by Emir Leiss. He was joined by Della Tallis' twelve Mudirs and by Cyrus and Navid, who were allowed in as witnesses to Roxanne's capture. Leiss, Taja and several others in the room had seen their last winter and might begin the swift disintegration into death at any moment. In the meantime, they had a duty to perform – and duty was one of those Long Dead concepts that the Constants clung to ferociously.

"Right," said the Emir, standing squarely before the fireplace, "I'll begin by asking Taja to explain what has been going on."

The Mudir of the West Tower outlined the events of earlier that day. She did not, however, mention that it was only after Cyrus' plea that she had taken the decision to shoot the hunting dogs.

"And I requested a meeting of the Majlis, Emir," she concluded, "because we have no idea who this woman is. She says she's one of us, a Constant, yet she carries the mark of a Zed. I believe we must be very, very careful. Even if she was once a Constant, who's to say she has not turned traitor and tricked her way in here to betray us to the Zeds?"

"And what do you recommend, Taja?" Leiss asked.

Taja turned from the Emir and, glancing quickly at Cyrus, said firmly, "Simple. We must take no risks. If at the end of this meeting there remains any shadow of a doubt in our minds, the Z-marked woman who calls herself Roxanne has to be executed."

At these words, the room filled with a buzz of whispered conversation. It was typical of Taja to be so forthright, and in nine cases out of ten her judgement, however harsh, proved correct. Nevertheless, Cyrus felt uneasy. There was something other than reasonable caution in Taja's attitude towards the good-looking stranger. He sensed what it was, too, although he

21

didn't want to admit it.

Leiss raised a hand. "Quiet please. I hear what you say, Taja, and this is what we will do. We'll hear Roxanne's story from her own mouth. When she has finished, we will take a handshow. If, after listening to her, nine or more of us decide she can be trusted, we will accept her into our community. If not, we will execute her. Agreed?"

There was a murmur of assent.

At Leiss' command, Cyrus and Navid went outside and returned with Roxanne. With a grace that was almost noble, she nodded respectfully to the Emir before taking her place across the table from him. Taja confirmed the prisoner's identity, drawing the company's attention to the livid Z-shaped tattoo on her forehead.

Leiss nodded. "Thank you, Taja. Right, Roxanne – or whoever you are – what have you to say?"

While she gathered her thoughts, the prisoner looked steadily around the room. That morning she had been running for her life. Now, barely into the afternoon, she was being asked to argue for her life. It would not be easy. She was among strange people. Constants, yes, but from a community that had developed differently from hers, people with their own customs and ways of thinking. Comparing their plain rough clothing with her own tattered yet still brightly coloured tunic, she noted that the Tallins were technically less advanced than those among whom she had grown up.

Although she did not know it, Roxanne faced another, far more serious difficulty. The arrival of an outsider had electrified

22

the people of Della Tallis, but it had also frightened them. Behind the fifteen pairs of eyes fixed upon her lingered a dark suspicion of betrayal.

"I come from a community of Constants like yours," Roxanne began. "Its name is Yonne and it's many, many miles from here."

"What's that?" interrupted Leiss. "What is 'miles'?"

"My apologies, Emir. 'Miles' is a word from the time of the Long Dead. It means a certain distance."

"How far?"

"Around one thousand paces, I think."

Leiss looked confused. "You've run many thousands of paces from this Yonne place?"

What Roxanne did next convinced Cyrus that she was no Zed. She smiled. It was not a broad grin but a simple, slight movement of the lips that brightened her whole face and brought a sparkle to her tired green eyes. That one look spoke more eloquently to Cyrus, and several others in the room, than all the words that followed.

There was one particular thing about Yonne, Roxanne explained, that made it different from Della Tallis. Did they know of 'paper'? Leiss nodded. Well, she went on, after the Great Death survivors burned nearly all paper for fuel. Somehow, almost miraculously, the Yonners' ancestors had managed to preserve three books. These were now valuable relics, locked away and seen by only the élite of each generation.

"And I am one of those who have seen the books," Roxanne said, adding slowly, "I can read and write."

23

Once again muttering filled the room. The Tallins were illiterate. Nevertheless, despite never having seen one, they knew the word "book". To them it was a source of wonder and truth, like an oracle, and books featured in some of their legends. They knew of writing, too, because they found it on ancient objects. But no one knew how to read. And now this brave and attractive outsider had turned up claiming to be able to decipher those mysterious markings!

"Prove it!" interrupted a tall, lean man with a hooked nose. He walked over to Roxanne, drew a knife from his belt and handed it to her. "The Long Dead made this knife," he explained. "It has some of this writing on the blade. Look! What does it mean?"

Taking the knife, Roxanne wiped it on the sleeve of her tunic and looked at the shining metal. "It is very worn, but I can make out some words. It says, *Stai...Stainless Steel. Made in...*I don't know this word, but I think it's *Taiwan*. It then says *two thousand and thirteen*."

These words from the olive-skinned stranger appeared to mesmerise the Majlis. Despite her hideous tattoo, torn clothing and scratched limbs, she was like a prophet from a higher civilisation. If the handshow had been taken at that moment, she would have been instantly accepted.

Taja brought them back down to earth. "Very clever," she retorted. "Yet many things worry me about you, Roxanne. We still don't know whether you're telling the truth, do we? Anyone can make up words. Why, for example, would someone put the words 'two thousand and thirteen' on a knife? Did you just invent that number?"

Roxanne remained calm. "A good question, Taja," she replied, turning to face her challenger. "I quite understand why you want to know. I think the number tells us when the knife was made. What we call 'winters' they called 'years'. This knife was made in the year two thousand and thirteen. The Yonners have kept a record of the winters since the Great Death and, using the Long Dead way of counting, it is now the year two thousand, one hundred and six."

"Two thousand, one hundred and six?" Leiss asked slowly. "What's that mean? Is it the number of winters since the beginning of the world?"

Roxanne shook her head. "I'm sorry, Emir, but I don't know."

"Useless information, then!" cut in Taja.

"Maybe," Roxanne shrugged. "But it might be helpful one day. If we were to find the Soterion." She looked round to see whether her audience understood what she was talking about. Frowns and puzzled expressions gave her the answer.

Moving over to lean wearily against a table, Roxanne outlined the legend of the Soterion. A group of Long Dead, seeing their world falling apart, had decided to preserve its knowledge for future generations. They collected hundreds of books and papers which they stored deep underground, safe from the weather and Zed vandalism. They named this vault the "Soterion". Yonners believed it was still there, waiting to be discovered.

"Whoever finds it," Roxanne concluded, looking round the silent room, "will gain the knowledge of the Long Dead – making iron and medicine and a thousand other things. As long as they can read."

"Like you," said Taja. "Very convenient!"

Roxanne sighed. "Yes, like me. But there is something else. Yonner folklore also tells how the cleverest of the Long Dead had been working on what they called the Salvation Project, a cure for the Great Death. They died before the medicine was ready, but a record of their work was among the last pieces of information placed in the Soterion as it was being sealed.

"If we had those writings," Roxanne continued, rising to her feet and speaking in a voice that trembled with excitement, "If we had those writings and the knowledge of the Long Dead, perhaps we could make that medicine. Then we would not die after our eighteenth winter as we do now, but grow old slowly, living for many, many years. Think what that would mean for our children, for our grandchildren. Yes, you would live long enough to see and hold your own grandchildren in your arms!"

When the Majlis had calmed down after this extraordinary speech, Leiss asked Roxanne what the Soterion story had to do with her.

"It's why I'm here," she explained, pushing back her hair so that her Zed scar was revealed in dreadful clarity. In the spring, Yonne had welcomed visitors from the Constant settlement of Alba. The Albans, who like the Tallins were illiterate, claimed to have found a sort of man-made cave set into the side of the mountain where they lived. Although unable to get inside, an image cut into the rusting steel door had interested them greatly: they thought it might be a book.

The door was engraved with words, too. Alban craft workers

had copied the markings by carving them on pieces of wood, and these were presented to the Yonners. Imagine the delight of both groups of Constants when it was confirmed that the image was indeed that of a book and the words beneath it read "The Soterion".

Six literate Yonners – Roxanne among them – volunteered to return to Alba to teach reading and, it was hoped, find a way into the fabled Soterion.

"You volunteered?" cut in Taja, her eyes narrowing.

"Yes. Why does it matter?"

"As we were bringing you here, I thought you said you had two children?"

Roxanne hesitated. "I do. It was not easy. But they are well cared for back in Yonne, and sometimes the community is more important than the individual."

"Of course." Taja's voice was sharp, almost bitter. "Go on."

"I had a chance to do something great, perhaps to change the lives of all Constants everywhere, for ever. It was my duty to go. Besides, my eighteenth winter has passed, so my children will lose me soon anyway."

Roxanne turned and looked calmly at Taja. "Wouldn't you have done the same?"

There was no reply. As everyone in the room except Roxanne knew, Taja was childless.

Roxanne resumed her story, saying how excited the whole Yonne community was when the Soterion Mission set out. It would only be a matter of time, they believed, before the great day would come, the day when the Soterion would yield up the knowledge of the Long Dead – and perhaps news of the Salvation Project, too.

It was not to be. The small band was ambushed by Zeds. As was their custom, the barbarians killed the men, reserving just one for their ghastly ritual. Two women were slain in the attack. The surviving two, Roxanne and an hysterical Alban woman, were raped and tortured. They were then tattooed with Zs and kept as slaves. Worse still, the leader of the tribe singled Roxanne out for special attention. She did not spell out exactly what he had done but confessed that, under torture, she had told him about the Soterion.

Roxanne paused, distressed by the memory of what she had been through. Eventually she added, "Fortunately, I managed to escape before telling him where it was."

"How did you get away?" asked the youngest of the Mudirs, staring wide-eyed at his new hero. He couldn't imagine the Zeds letting anyone out of their clutches.

"There are ways," Roxanne replied coolly. "All men, even Zeds, have their weaknesses."

When Taja greeted this remark with a snort of contempt, Roxanne gave her a curious look. It spoke more of compassion than anger, Cyrus noted. She certainly was a remarkable woman.

The rest of her story, Roxanne concluded, they already knew. With the Zeds closing in on her fast, she had stumbled upon the Della Tallis community quite by accident. Even then, she would have been ripped to pieces before reaching safety if Taja had not told the archers to shoot the dogs.

"There we are. That's who I am and why I'm here," concluded

Roxanne, suddenly looking thoroughly exhausted. "I know it must sound strange, almost impossible. But it is true, I promise you. If you believe me, I beg you to give me an escort so that I may continue my mission to Alba."

"Right," said Leiss quickly. He did not want further discussion in Roxanne's presence. "Cyrus and Navid, take the prisoner outside again while we decide what to do with her."

Instinctively, Cyrus took hold of Roxanne's arm. She turned towards him, half smiling. "Not necessary, Cyrus. I'm not going to try to escape, am I? I'm too tired and there's nowhere for me to go."

Cyrus withdrew his hand and followed Navid and Roxanne out of the room. What was it, he wondered, that made this woman so different? Unlike anyone he had met, she seemed to command affection and respect in equal measure from complete strangers.

As soon as the prisoner had left, Leiss invited the Mudirs to give their opinion. The hook-nosed man who had spoken earlier was the first to catch the Emir's eye. "We're born, we live, we die," he growled. "That's the way it is. Doesn't seem right to me to try to find a way to live for forty, fifty or even a hundred winters."

"The Long Dead did," interrupted Obadis, a fair-haired man who had lost an eye in a shooting accident. "And they were cleverer than us, Rustam. They built this house for a start."

"Maybe," Rustam replied. "But that was them and we are us. Different. That Roxanne woman seemed alright to me, but I don't want her trying to change things, that's all."

This annoyed Zuleyka, the excitable Mudir of the Central Tower. "You're not thinking straight, Rustam," she said, pumping her hands up and down in frustration. "If we lived another ten winters, we'd see our children grow to ten or twelve winters themselves – then think what we'd be able to pass on to them: all our ideas, all we have learned. They wouldn't have to learn everything all over again."

"And we're Constants, aren't we?" added her friend Vashti. "We're loyal to the ways of the Long Dead. We want to be like them, not Zeds."

After the discussion had ranged backwards and forwards for a while, Azat, the one Mudir who had not yet spoken suddenly thumped his fist on the table. "Listen!" he roared, glaring about him. "As you know, I'm a fighter not a talker. But fighters know one thing. Never, ever trust a Zed! I should know, shouldn't I?"

To emphasise this remark, Azat pointed to the jagged pits and scars that disfigured the whole of the left side of his face. Three years before, he had escaped from a Zed ambush with an axe embedded below his eye. It was a testament to his ox-like strength that the hideous blow had not killed him.

"That fancy woman's got you like fish on a hook, hasn't she? Bah! Lies! She's all lies. She's got the mark, hasn't she? That's all you need to know. Kill her!"

Taja broke the silence that followed this harangue. "As Azat says, the Z-marked woman spoke very well, very convincingly. But maybe she was too convincing?

"As must be clear to you by now, like Azat, I do not trust her. The chase, the dogs…it could all have been set up. We have no proof, just the word of a stranger, a stranger with the mark of our enemies. Are you really going to risk everything for that?"

"Never!" grunted Azat, fingering his scar.

Taja nodded. "There's something else. Surely we all know the story of the Four?"

A general murmur of assent ran round the room.

The story of the Tallins' last meeting with Constants from other settlements was semi-legendary. Some twenty-four moons ago, four outsiders, all exhausted and suffering from ghastly wounds, had crawled up to the outer barricade one night and begged to be allowed in. They survived only a few days, but before dying they had told how a traitor Constant had betrayed their remote settlement to the Zeds. It was looted, then burned. The children were slaughtered and women over the age of eleven taken away as breeding slaves. Some of the men were burned alive in the buildings; others – about two dozen – were saved for the Zeds' most grizzly ritual of triumph.

This involved, the men reported, a great fire with a red-hot metal spit suspended above it. After much wild dancing and chanting, one of the captives was led forward and stripped of his clothes. At this point, while the Zeds were distracted by their hideous rite, the four had made a run for it. They had not seen for certain what the fire and the spit had been for, but they had witnessed enough to imagine.

"You hardly need me to tell you what this tale means," said Taja. "The Four's community had been handed over to the Zeds by a traitor. Similarly, the greatest threat to us is not a direct Zed attack but betrayal from within. Can you be absolutely sure this

31

Roxanne is not a spy? If we let her go, won't she report back on the way we defend ourselves, on our points of weakness? Not all Zeds are stupid, you know."

"Spy!" interrupted Azat. "Yes, that's it. Too clever by half. She's a spy, or my name's not Azat."

"Maybe," replied Taja. "We can't be certain. But that's the point. Listen, do you honestly want to risk our whole settlement because some branded woman comes in here and spins a yarn about secrets hidden in a cave in a place we've never heard of thousands and thousands of paces away?"

Taja paused. Looking round the room at each person in turn, she concluded slowly, "Think about it, fellow Mudirs. For all our sakes, think about it."

"We will. Thank you, Taja," said Leiss with a frown. The decision did not now seem as straightforward as it had moments before.

The Emir walked slowly to the fireplace and once again raised a hand for silence. "Right. We have heard enough. It's time for the handshow."

2
Into the Unknown

Navid closed the door of the Prison Hut and leaned heavily against it. "Well, Cy?"

His friend was drawing idly in the dust with the point of his spear. "Well, what?"

"Come on!" Born on the same day sixteen winters ago and close friends all their lives, the two young men read each other's thoughts as easily as they read the weather. "You know what I mean, Cy. How d'you think the handshow will go?"

"Most of them are sharp enough to see she's telling the truth."

"Taja's the sharpest of the lot, and she didn't believe a word Roxanne said."

Cyrus angrily crossed out the pattern he had drawn. "Maybe."

Navid's brain did not match the speed of his powerful warrior's body. "What's that supposed to mean?"

"You know, Nav. It's general knowledge how Taja and I have been since Pari died. And once she's set her mind on something, someone…So, it's not as simple as whether she believes Roxanne or not. There we were, getting along OK, and then this stranger turns up. Taja sensed a threat almost immediately." He hesitated, as if trying to make sense of his own thoughts. "You must admit, Nav," he continued, speaking more slowly, "Roxanne's quite, well, unusual, isn't she?"

Navid grinned. "Really?" Typical Cyrus! Too much heart for his own good. At one time or another he had fancied just about every woman in Della Tallis. A merry dance he'd led them till he settled down with Pari, his wedun; and now it looked as if it might start all over again. Except this time, if the refugee was involved, it would be a lot more serious – and a lot more dangerous.

Cyrus smiled back at his friend but said nothing. Since Pari's death in childbirth, Taja had made it clear that she wanted Cyrus for herself. She was certainly an attractive woman. He liked and respected her, and the two had spent several nights together. Even so, he had nagging doubts about the relationship. He was no good at pretending and her intensity made the affair lopsided and sometimes awkward. He also worried that she might be more interested in what he was – a handsome man destined for high authority – than who he was. Having seen her final winter, she was no longer able to bear a child and likely to enter her Death Month at any moment. Custom and common sense told Cyrus he should find a wedun younger than himself, one capable of producing the children desperately needed to keep the community going.

And now there was Roxanne, complicating things still further.

The sound of the farmhouse door opening interrupted Cyrus' thoughts. Mudir Vashti came blinking into the sunlight. The two men searched her face for a clue as to how the handshow had gone. Strangely, for Vashti was one of the most open women in all Della Tallis, their unspoken question received no answer. She neither frowned nor smiled. Her taut face conveyed nothing but a vague sense of uncertainty.

"Well, Vashti, what's been decided?"

"I can't tell you, Cyrus. Emir Leiss wants the prisoner back in the Majlis so she can hear the verdict for herself."

Navid opened the door of the Hut and peered inside. "Roxanne?" he called quietly. "You're wanted back in the Majlis."

There was no reply. Exhausted by the events of the night, the plaintiff had curled up in a corner of the hut and fallen asleep. Navid entered and shook her by the shoulder.

The sleeping woman flinched. "No, Timur! No! Please!" The voice was one the onlookers had not heard before. Half begging, half screaming, it chilled the very air that carried it, sweeping away any lingering doubt the two Defenders might have had about her honesty. Her dream – her nightmare – was thick with horrors. They woke her gently and led her back to face the Majlis.

The atmosphere in the room was uneasy, as if the handshow had not yet taken place. Cyrus glanced around. As he had done with Vashti, he scanned the faces of the Mudirs for a hint of the decision. Nothing. All of them had their eyes fixed on the Emir, as if only he knew the result.

"Roxanne," Leiss began, his dark face furrowed with seriousness, "we agreed that if nine of us trust you, you may remain in Della Tallis. If fewer than nine believe your story, you will be executed."

As the Emir paused, Cyrus glanced towards the prisoner. She stood absolutely still, eyes fixed on the speaker. Only a slight twitching of her fingers revealed her nervousness. On the other side of the table, Taja swept a strand of hair from her face. The movement caught Cyrus' attention and, as she intended, his eyes flicked in her direction. Slowly, with the suggestion of a pout, she mouthed the word "execute".

Cyrus looked away, wishing he had not understood.

"Roxanne, the Majlis has held its handshow," Leiss continued. "The majority of the Mudirs believe you are to be trusted. However, four of them – Rustam, Azat, Ebi and Taja – were not convinced by your story. That makes the count eight to four."

Cyrus felt anger swelling within him. He wanted to shout, to tell those who had not supported the refugee how blind and stupid they were. How could they have let themselves be persuaded by Taja when her motives were patently mixed? He took a deep breath and glared across at her. She met his gaze without blinking.

Turning away in frustration, Cyrus saw that Roxanne had begun to weep. She didn't heave or shake. Rather, she stood quite still as if unaware of the tears running silently down her face and splashing heavily onto her chest. Cyrus bit his lip in an effort to control his emotions. Navid, also aware of the mounting tension, gripped the handle of his axe more tightly. At his feet,

Corby let out a low growl. Even the dog, it seemed, sensed that the Constant traditions of loyalty and obedience were being stretched to breaking point.

Dangerous thoughts flashed through Cyrus' mind, thoughts he had never known he was capable of. One did not reject the result of a handshow. To do so would be to undermine every principle of the Constants' fragile society, feeding dangerous division, perhaps rebellion…Yet how dumb would it be to kill someone bearing a message of almost unbelievable hope? Maybe, at moments like this, they needed something more than constancy and blind obedience.

Through the mist of his confusion, Cyrus became aware that Leiss was still speaking. Something about one more handshow. Of course! The Emir himself had not yet given his opinion. Cyrus's attention switched back to what was being said.

"Roxanne, you see what a difficult position you have put me in? Your fate is in my hands." Leiss looked down at the floor then stared for a few seconds at the refugee's tear-stained face. "I share many of Taja's fears. Indeed, before you came back in I was going to recommend your execution. Your reaction to what you have heard has saved you. Tears do not move me, but dignity does. You are too dignified for a Zed. Therefore, I add my choice to the eight cast in your favour, making nine."

In the bustle of conversation that greeted the Emir's verdict, Cyrus and Navid nodded to each other in relief. Ignoring them, Taja stared hawk-eyed at the woman she had sought to condemn.

Leiss called for quiet. "Nevertheless," he went on, "because of the worries expressed by Taja and others, it would be wrong to provide Roxanne with an escort for her journey. In fact, she must remain here for a whole moon so we can keep an eye on her. Just in case. After that, Roxanne, if you wish to continue your mission, you'll have to go alone. On those conditions, therefore, Roxanne the Yonner, welcome to Della Tallis!"

A shadow had passed over Roxanne's face as she listened to Leiss' judgement. Cyrus saw it and understood immediately. So also, he feared, had Taja. The Emir may have saved the striking Yonner's life, but he had also put a stop to her mission. Cyrus realised that his constancy was again going to be put to the test, and he was unsure how he would react.

When the noise had subsided, Leiss asked Cyrus and Navid to leave. He wanted to say something to Roxanne and the Majlis in confidence. Cyrus learned later that the Emir was understandably worried about the Mudirs' disagreements leaving deeper, long-lasting divisions within the community. Whatever their individual opinions, he reminded everyone, they had to accept the result of the handshow and put their differences behind them. Duty demanded unity at all times.

Roxanne thanked the Majlis and the Emir in particular. She quite understood the fears of those who had not believed her, she added, and would do her best to work for Della Tallis and Constants everywhere. Of those present, only Taja noticed how carefully the words were chosen. Leiss then invited all the Mudirs to come forward and shake the visitor's hand as a gesture of goodwill. When this small ceremony was over, Vashti and Zuleyka accompanied Roxanne to their dormitory so she could clean herself up and rest.

Cyrus did not see Roxanne for the rest of the day. Nor did he see Taja. As soon as Navid and he were dismissed from the meeting, they joined a party strengthening the central watchtower and the barricades on either side of it. The manual work served to calm the turmoil in Cyrus' brain.

For as long as he could remember, he had tried to do what was right, to behave as expected from someone with his obvious talents. Although no angel, he had done his best to serve the community and treat everyone with respect. But now, with the arrival of Roxanne, the focus had shifted. His personal life and his role in the community were suddenly, painfully less straightforward. Instinct drew him towards Roxanne and the news of the Soterion; his upbringing told him that only fools or traitors threw away the present in the vague hope of a better future.

"Know why we're called Constants, Nav?" he asked, trying to sound as casual as possible as he hauled another pole to the top of the watchtower.

"Eh?"

"Constant – why are we 'Constants' rather than, say, 'Valiants' or 'Fighters'?"

"How should I know, Cy? You're the one with the brains." Navid leaned against the rail that ran around the top of the tower. "It's because we are, I suppose."

"Are what, Nav?"

"You know, constant. Not changing, reliable, like the sun coming up every morning."

"And going down every evening," muttered Cyrus.

Sensitive to his friend's anxiety, Navid decided not to take the conversation any further. This Roxanne business was Cyrus' affair, something only he could sort out. If, when he did so, he needed help, Navid would stand beside him. Until then, he would say nothing. The first move had to come from Cy.

Beyond the defences on which Cyrus and Navid were working, a party of young men and women was harvesting apples in open ground. It was dangerous work. Every two or three moons, an "outside picker", as they were known, would be carried off in a lightning Zed raid. To guard against this, lookouts scanned the steep walls of the valley, ready to recall the pickers at the first sign of enemy movement.

On this occasion they need not have worried. There were indeed Zeds within the distant trees, but at that moment they were more concerned with punishment than the recapture of a prisoner.

The scene was an ugly one. A naked Zed of some fifteen winters was tied to a tree with a length of frayed rope. Around him, some standing transfixed, some clutching themselves in delight, were forty or so unshaven, barbaric-looking men. These were common Zeds, barely articulate, barely human. They obeyed only their animal instincts and the commands of their leader. The spectacle of punishment fascinated them.

The victim was one of their own number. His body was a mass of fresh and bloody wounds, many where the flesh was most tender and most sensitive. The bleeding was heaviest from his mouth in which only half a dozen broken teeth remained.

The others lay scattered across the ground in front of him like a miniature graveyard from the time of the Long Dead.

The image was appropriate. Soon this man would be dead, too. Before then he was going to suffer. He would suffer for not guarding his prisoner closely enough and for failing to recapture her. He would also suffer simply to give pleasure to his tormentors.

"Teeth!" hissed a high voice. "The vermin still has teeth! It might bite me!"

A young Zed clad in a short kilt of hide stepped forward and brandished a thin iron spike in front of the prisoner's face.

"No!" came the voice again. "Lever them out slowly, Sheza. Don't simply smash them! Enjoy!"

Sheza was being educated. Today's lesson, in the art of torture, was being given by the teacher who sat on the ground a few paces behind him, calling out instructions.

A scream tore through the trees as another two teeth dropped to the forest floor.

"That's better. But what a noise it makes! I think it's time for the tongue, don't you?"

From his haughty bearing, his sneering expression of cold command and his multicoloured cloak, it was clear that the instructor was no ordinary Zed. He was none other than Timur the Terrible, leader – or "Malik" – of the self-styled Grozny, the most formidable of all the Zed tribes. Timur's cruelty was renowned, even among his own kind. So was his intelligence. From the age of twelve, when he was appointed Malik by his predecessor, he had been accustomed to having his way with

41

every man, woman and child he came across.

Until he met Roxanne.

Timur had made her suffer, of course. At the same time, he had been intrigued by her striking looks and dignified personality. He decided, therefore, not to kill her but to tattoo her as a Zed and keep her as his personal plaything. She flattered him and grew close to where his heart would have been, had he possessed one. He also kept her alive for a more practical reason. When tortured to tell the purpose of her mission, she had talked of the Soterion. Timur had heard of reading and books, and realised they could be a source of knowledge. And knowledge was power, power to crush the Constants and extend his rule to the very sea itself.

The Zeds under his command would not understand this. So what? He had no time for them. They were mere brutes while he, Malik Timur, was different. He was like one of those things he had heard an Alban Constant call upon under torture. What was it? Ah, yes! A god. That was it. He was like a god.

But he was not yet a god. If he were, he would never have let Roxanne wheedle her way out of his grip before she had revealed where the Soterion was. Now he would never know… Or would he? Maybe, just maybe, all was not lost after all…

Timur thoughtfully fingered his wispy beard and returned to the business in hand. "Haven't you removed the tongue yet? Oh, Sheza! You must do that before we get down to the really amusing part."

Whether he recaptured Roxanne or not, Timur would make an unforgettable example of the batbrained idiot he held

42

responsible for letting her go. If he did not, it was possible that some of his sharper followers might suspect the truth. Roxanne's escape had been his fault.

The next day, Roxanne slipped out of the Mudir dormitory as night was falling and made her way to the bridge that lay between the settlement and its fields. She was less tired now and less conspicuous in a simple Tallin dress of plain wool. This was the first time she had been left alone since the meeting of the Majlis, and she had to make the most of it. Her Death Month drew closer by the day, blotting out the horizon like an approaching storm.

On the bridge she paused, looked around to make sure she was alone, and gazed at her reflection in the clear water below. Long hair, almost black, framed a face of high cheekbones and brilliant green eyes. Above, jagged and crude, the disfiguring mark of a Zed. She raised a hand and traced the scar with her fingers.

"Yes, it was the cruellest, cleverest thing he could have done, wasn't it?" She recognised the voice at once. So he had been watching for her, as she hoped. She had not overestimated him.

"Cyrus. I'm glad you've come. Thank you."

He left her and walked on over the bridge without looking back. "Not here, Roxanne. It's too public. Someone's bound to be watching."

The remark was truer than he realised.

Roxanne waited till Cyrus had disappeared into the trees flanking the path, then crossed the bridge herself and turned right. After a short walk, she came to a place where the river bank had fallen in, creating a low beach beside the stream. Here she waited, listening intently.

Cyrus found her shortly afterwards. Calling her name quietly from the top of the bank, he scrambled down to stand before her in the darkness.

"Roxanne, I wanted to speak to you because, well…"

"I know, Cyrus," she interrupted, speaking with a quiet urgency. "You believed in me from the beginning, from the moment I came over your barricade, and I'm so grateful to you. I won't let you down, I promise. You know I need assistance, don't you? Whatever Leiss says, I have to get away soon. And I can't manage on my own."

Cyrus' sensitive face with defined, even features, handsome in daylight, struck her as even more attractive by starlight. She took half a step back. No, she told herself, there can be no complications. She would soon be dead, and then nothing would matter. Before that, she must reach the Soterion.

"I have been through it in my mind dozens of times, Roxanne. Of course I want to help you. But Leiss forbade us from going with you. You are asking a Constant to disobey his Emir, to break the principles of a lifetime."

"Lifetimes are short, Cyrus, and not all principles are equal. Might your duty to all Constants be greater than to just those of Della Tallis?"

"Maybe. If I knew for certain you are what you say and Taja is wrong to mistrust you…"

"Taja? Well, only you can make that decision, Cyrus."

44

They remained there for some time, side by side, gazing at the starlight on the black surface of the stream. When Cyrus eventually spoke, he found it difficult to keep the tremor out of his voice.

"Alright, Roxanne. Count me in. Your mission has just doubled in size."

His hand reached out in the darkness and grasped hers. She did not withdraw.

Cyrus had been on a number of forays out of Della Tallis. Some were scavenging expeditions, collecting remains from the time of the Long Dead; others were military operations to drive back nomadic Zeds camped too close to the settlement's boundary. He had no trouble, therefore, in drawing up a plan to get out unchallenged.

Inviting other warriors to join him was trickier. He could approach only those he trusted absolutely. At the same time, he did not want to put his friends in a difficult position by forcing them to choose between keeping his secret and their loyalty to the community. He was, after all, asking them to disobey the Emir's express command. The punishment for that was death.

Navid was the obvious choice. Even so, Cyrus hesitated. To his surprise, it was his friend who ended the agonising.

"To save you asking, yes, I will," Navid said suddenly on the afternoon following Cyrus' pact with Roxanne.

"Eh?"

"Come on, Cy. I might be slow but I'm not Zed speed."

"What do you mean?"

"Roxanne's had her eighteenth winter, yes?"

"Yes. I think that's right."

"You know it is, Cy. Her Death Month can't be that far away, and it's pretty obvious she's not going to wait here until it starts. She's a woman on a mission."

"Is it that obvious, Nav?"

Navid grinned. "Well, I worked it out so others probably have. And I also worked out that she can't do it alone. She needs companions, helpers. So I asked myself, 'Navid, who do you think she would turn to?' Answer, clear as a dew drop: Cyrus."

"I see. But you can't come, Nav. What about Salama? She will have your second baby soon." He was fond of Navid's wedun and did not want to be responsible for separating the couple.

"She agrees. I've told her."

"You what?!" cried Cyrus, looking round to see if anyone was listening. "Nav, you didn't –"

"Hey, don't worry! All I said was that if I was to leave on some incredibly important mission, would she mind? Well, you know Salama. She said straight away it was up to me. No questions asked."

Although Cyrus was not sure that she really grasped what was suggested, this was not the time for quibbling. If Navid had guessed that Roxanne was going to ask others to join her on the mission, who else might have reached the same conclusion? Leiss, perhaps. Certainly Taja. Cyrus looked around again, anxiously. They had to go that very night.

The two men agreed immediately on who should be the third warrior in the party. Zavar was the finest swordsman of his generation, wielding his steel blade with dazzling skill, and he was also terrifyingly brave. A few months ago, he had rescued a fellow Defender by charging alone into a band of Zeds and slaying all eight of them. Now in his final year of life but still on the lookout for fresh adventure, he instantly accepted Cyrus' invitation to join them.

So it was that shortly before dawn the following morning, a band of four Defenders, tightly wrapped up against the cold and accompanied by a large dog, approached the watchtower manned by Obadis. Cyrus greeted the one-eyed Mudir cheerfully, explaining that he was leading a small scouting party to check that the Zeds who had pursued Roxanne had now left the district.

Obadis hesitated. No one had told him about this patrol and he was not supposed to let anyone out without express permission from Leiss. "He said we should keep an eye open for this Roxanne woman," he explained with unconscious irony, "in case she tries to break out before a moon has passed."

"Roxanne?" laughed Cyrus. "You reckon she'd want to go out into Zed territory again after what she's been through? Be sensible, Obadis!"

The Mudir nodded and ordered the Defenders in his sector to let the scouting party pass. Not long afterwards, the four figures had cleared the barricade and, with the dog loping along behind, disappeared into the morning mist. "Hope they know what they're doing," Obadis muttered to himself.

He was surprised when, a few seconds later, a familiar figure glided into view and asked him the same question. Did he know what he was doing?

Obadis hesitated, inwardly cursing his poor eyesight. All of a sudden he was unsure how to reply.

By sunrise, the mission had crossed the open land surrounding Della Tallis and reached the safety of the woods further up the valley. The men, sure that no Tallin would pursue them this far, relaxed and started congratulating themselves on how easy it had been. Roxanne was less cheerful. She was fearful about being back in Zed territory and also anxious about the route they should take.

The Albans had said the way back to the Soterion lay in the direction of the rising sun. Part of the trail followed a Long Dead freeway that the Yonners identified as Highway 24. Although direct, the road was also highly dangerous; much of its length lay across arid semi-desert where food and water were hard to come by. Following this route would be tough enough, but first they had to find it. That meant striking out across unknown territory where vicious bands of scavenging Zeds lurked amid the overgrown ruins of abandoned towns.

After her capture, Roxanne had only a rough idea of where Timur had taken her. The sun had been at her back, she thought. There had also been a river, a huge one that the Zeds had crossed with some difficulty. She suggested, therefore, that they set out in the opposite direction to the one in which she had been taken as a prisoner. By journeying towards the sun at its highest – "noon" the Long Dead had called it – they should meet either the river or Highway 24.

"Before we go any further," she added, glancing round at her escort, "there is something else you need to know." The men looked at her intently. "You dismiss the Zeds as stupid. Well, nearly all of them are – little more than dumb brutes. But they are kept like that by their leaders. These men – and they are all men – are a carefully chosen élite, all surprisingly intelligent.

"The cleverest of all – and without doubt the most evil – is the man they call their 'Malik'. His name is –"

"Timur," interrupted Cyrus without thinking. "Sorry, Roxanne," he added quickly, "that's the name you cried out in your sleep on the day you arrived."

An expression of pain moved across Roxanne's face. "Yes, Cyrus, his name is Timur. And unless I have misjudged him, he will have been waiting for me to leave Della Tallis and continue my mission."

Zavar let out a low whistle. "You mean they're coming to us rather than us having to go looking for them?" he chuckled. "That makes a change!"

"Maybe," frowned Roxanne, "but take great care. I have already fallen victim to one of Timur's ambushes once." She gave a slight shudder. "It's not an experience I want to repeat."

Cyrus, who had assumed leadership of the party, accepted all Roxanne said. He arranged for Navid and Corby to lead the way – the dog's acute senses would alert them to danger long before they were aware of it themselves. He would follow, with Roxanne and Zavar bringing up the rear. Where possible, they would travel on high ground where an ambush was harder to organise. First, though, they had to get out of the valley.

Moving as quietly as possible and keeping to Cyrus' formation, the Constants set off up the slope. They had gone no more than a few hundred paces when Corby began to growl and sniff around a clump of thick scrub to their left. Navid went to investigate. Standing in front of Roxanne with his spear at the ready, Cyrus watched and waited.

From behind him, Roxanne's voice splintered the silence. "Cyrus!"

He spun round to see a Zed warrior, javelin raised, a couple of paces away. The man couldn't miss. He tensed his arm for the throw – then suddenly it went limp. The javelin dropped harmlessly to the ground, followed by the quivering body of the Zed himself. A Constant arrow, fired with lethal precision, stuck out from his neck like a quill. Blood pumped from the wound and spread in a crimson pool across the sandy soil.

Cyrus stared open-mouthed at the archer who had saved his life. Impossible! Not here…How did she…?

"I thought I'd join you," Taja said calmly, lowering her bow, "to make sure you knew what you were doing, Cyrus. I also wanted to keep an eye on Roxanne – you know what I feel about her, don't you?"

No one replied.

Taja drew level with Zavar. "You may be a fine swordsman," she said icily, "but you're useless at fieldcraft. I've been following you ever since you deceived Obadis. Poor man! I hope they don't execute him."

After a painful pause, Cyrus said quietly. "Thank you, Taja.

You just saved my life."

Taja nodded. "Like I saved Roxanne's when I ordered the dogs to be shot. Now you both owe me – kindly don't forget it."

"This isn't really the time for point scoring," cut in Roxanne. "That man you killed was not alone. We must get out… "

The sentence was never finished. Ignoring what was going on behind him, Corby continued rooting through the scrub. All of a sudden, he began to bark angrily. As if this was a signal, eight armed Zeds stood up in front of him.

At the same time, more warriors appeared from the trees on the other side of the track. Before the band of Constants had time to react, their enemies fanned out left and right.

Glancing around, Cyrus felt his throat run dry. They were surrounded.

"Well, Cyrus," said Navid quietly. "You're the leader. What now?"

3
Fighting Free

Cyrus was used to making quick decisions. For years, the Emirs of Della Tallis had singled him out as a future Mudir, and he had proved himself by leading a number of successful patrols out of Della Tallis. But he had never before been in such a desperate position.

Make a run for it or fight it out? The circling Zeds took a step closer. Eight to the left, four in front, and still more to the right and behind them…Twenty in total, all of them armed. No, a break out was impossible. Even if some of the Tallin party got through the ring, one of them was bound not to make it. What if it were Roxanne? If she went, the whole mission would be finished.

An urgent whisper broke into Cyrus' thoughts. "Give them Roxanne! Do a deal, Cyrus. Hand her over and they'll let us go!" It was Taja.

The words ran through Cyrus like an electric shock, jerking him into action. "Never!" he shouted, covering his response with a general order. "Constants never surrender! Shoulder to shoulder, and we'll show them what Tallin Defenders can do!"

The five – three men and two women – did as Cyrus commanded. Without a word, they came together in a tight knot of sinew and steel. At their feet, Corby snarled menacingly.

"Hold your positions, whatever happens," called Cyrus, his eyes fixed on the Zed standing directly before him. "Let them come to us."

At this, the Zed in front of Cyrus brandished his weapon, an evil-looking instrument known as a "gut-ripper", and began to speak: "Zed blood! Zed blood! Kill! Kill! Kill!"

Slowly and deliberately, he repeated the hypnotizing words. "Zed blood! Zed blood! Kill! Kill! Kill!"

The men on either side of him picked up the chant and the Tallins were soon surrounded by a frenzied circle of screaming, stamping barbarians. "Zed blood! Zed blood! Kill! Kill! Kill!" On and on it went, louder and louder, faster and faster, until the very trees seemed to join in the howling. "Zed blood! Zed blood! Kill! Kill! Kill!"

Cyrus glanced to his left. Roxanne – normally so calm, so composed – was quivering uncontrollably. She had seen all this before, he realized, and it must bring back unspeakable memories. He had to do something before she collapsed completely. Five against twenty would be hard enough; with just four, their task would be all but impossible.

Keeping his eyes fixed on the tall, bearded man in front of him, Cyrus slowly drew his knife from his belt. At the end of each verse, on the final "Kill!", he noticed that the Zed looked up at the sky and raised his arms above his head. At that moment, the scarred body, naked to the waist, was a perfect target.

A flash of bright steel, a slight whirring sound and then a dull thud as the knife struck home, burying itself deep into the man's stomach. "Zed blood! Zed blood! Kill…"

The chanting stopped as swiftly as it had begun. The woods were suddenly silent. All eyes turned to the man holding the gut-ripper as he stared in disbelief at the wooden handle projecting from his body. Then, to Cyrus' astonishment, with a ghastly grin he plucked the bloody dagger from his abdomen and flung it back towards the Tallins. It landed harmlessly a few feet in front of Roxanne.

The action broke the spell that held her. Keeping her eyes on the enemy, she bent down, picked the weapon up, wiped it on her tunic and handed it back to Cyrus. "Yours, I believe?" she said quietly. "I think you might need it."

No sooner were the words out of her mouth than the Zeds, infuriated by her composure and the injury to their leader, leaped forward with hideous cries of murder and revenge.

Four attackers fell before they reached the Tallins. After managing two short steps, the commander with the gut-ripper sagged to his knees clutching at the wound in his stomach. Blood seeped through his fingers and dripped to the ground. He never rose again. Three other Zeds were pierced by Taja's arrows. She shot with extraordinary rapidity, taking an arrow from her waist, fitting it to the bow, drawing and releasing it in what appeared to be a single movement. She aimed high, hitting two of her targets in the face and one in the chest.

Fortunately for the Constants, Timur had chosen the gut-ripper man as leader because of his ferocity, not his intelligence. He had told his band to leave their bows in the camp because they would be useless at close quarters. That left them armed only with a variety of crudely made spears, clubs and hooks, none of which was a match for the better-crafted Tallin weapons. Furthermore, the Zeds had come without dogs in case the half-trained beasts spoiled the surprise of an ambush – the Grozny had even less control over their animals than over themselves. Pain was their only discipline.

In short, unequal though the battle might have looked in terms of numbers, with five Zeds taken out before hand-to-hand combat began, the Tallins' position was not hopeless.

After the first exchanges, it looked even better. Wielding only wooden clubs, the Zeds who charged at Navid were no match for his mighty axe. The first lost an arm, the second died instantly when the blade sliced into his skull. Beside him, another man struggled in vain against the huge dog that pinned him to the ground by the throat. When it came to a fight, Corby was more than a match for any Zed.

To Navid's right, Cyrus fought off three opponents with his spear, stabbing one in the leg, another in the throat and a third with a well-aimed lunge to the chest.

Behind them, Zavar's sword flashed and twinkled in the broken sunlight filtering through the canopy of leaves. The two Zeds confronting him, unsure how to approach, darted this way and that trying to find a way in. Each time they advanced, they were pierced and sliced by that razor-sharp blade. Exhausted and bleeding heavily, they fell back.

Zavar was on the point of advancing to finish them off when he heard a cry to his left. It was Taja. Having fired all six arrows from her belt, she was trying desperately to defend herself with the long knife that all archers carried for cutting new ammunition. A Zed warrior armed with a club had knocked the weapon from her hand. Before her now loomed a grinning, broken-toothed warrior with a rusty machete poised above his head.

In one movement, Zavar spun round and drove forward with his sword. The Zed stood for a second, his expression frozen in deadly shock. An instant later, his machete clattered to the ground and he crumpled slowly beside it. Zavar's thrust had pierced his heart.

The club man made a second lunge at Taja as she stooped to retrieve her knife. With eyes fixed on his adversary, he failed to notice a quick movement to his right. The stainless steel bayonet Cyrus had given Roxanne before they set out slipped easily between the man's ribs. All Constants, young and old, male and female, were taught the skills of warfare: their lives depended on it. Roxanne was no exception.

Turning from the bayoneted man lying at her feet, Taja glanced towards the warrior whose swift action had saved her from serious injury, if not death. The eyes of the two women met. It was a glance of recognition, certainly, but Roxanne was unsure whether it was also a sign of reconciliation.

This was hardly the time for speculation. Zavar was in trouble. In turning to help Taja, he had momentarily taken his eyes off the Zeds immediately in front of him. Seizing his chance, a wiry fellow with the yellow tinge of jaundice upon his skin smashed his club into Zavar's left shoulder. The blow sent him reeling and, to regain his balance, he lowered his sword. At this, the second Zed stabbed him in the same shoulder with a barbed spike lashed to the end of a wooden pole. Hearing his cry of pain, the two women came to his rescue. Seconds later, both Zeds, already seriously weakened by Zavar's swordplay, were out of the fight.

No less than fourteen Zeds now lay bleeding upon the forest floor. Some were dead, others too badly injured to raise themselves. Cyrus appraised the situation in an instant. "Don't let even one get away!" he gasped. "Not a single one!"

The Tallins advanced carefully on the remaining Zeds. Corby brought down one, and Cyrus and Navid accounted for another two. Roxanne's bayonet gashed the back of a fourth as he fled into the trees with two other survivors. As giving chase risked another ambush, the exhausted Constants decided to let them go.

Navid, panting heavily, came over to Cyrus and put an arm round his shoulder. "Quite a fight, eh?" he grinned.

Cyrus brushed a lock of dark brown hair from his sweat-covered face. "Yes, but we shouldn't have let any escape, Nav. They know our position and will report back." He wiped the tip of his spear on a tuft of coarse grass. "We've got to get out of here quick, before they come after us with dogs."

First, though, they had to tend to Zavar. He was in great pain. The blow from the club had broken a bone in his shoulder and the wound from the spike was bleeding badly. He was able to walk, though. When Cyrus had fashioned a sling out of a belt and Roxanne had stopped the flow of blood with a pad of leaves and a woollen bandage, the party struck out in what they hoped was the direction of Highway 24. This time Roxanne and Navid led the way, followed by Zavar and Taja with Cyrus bringing up the rear. Corby, unhurt in the fray, trotted along happily beside his master.

At the top of the rise, the trees gave way to denser, more regular undergrowth that covered an ancient vineyard. One or two wild vines remained and the party eagerly grabbed the purple grapes as they hurried by. From time to time, Cyrus raised a hand and they paused to listen for the sound of dogs. Not till well into the afternoon did they hear the ominous barking echo up from the valley behind them. Faces furrowed with anxiety, they gathered under a broad-leafed beech to listen.

"Six, seven thousand paces away?" suggested Cyrus.

"Yeah, about that," nodded Navid.

Cyrus ran his hand through his hair. "Good. There's no way they'll catch up with us by sundown, and then they'll have to call off the hounds in case they lose them. We'll be safe in the dark."

Roxanne shook her head. "No, not safe, Cyrus. We'll never be safe from Timur as long as he's alive. I know the man only too well. He wants my secret and he'll pursue me, day and night, until he gets it."

"Then we'll stay ahead of him, Roxanne, and get to the

Soterion before he finds us. Trust me."

Cyrus looked towards Zavar, who was sitting with his back against the trunk of the tree. "How is it?" he asked, squatting down beside him.

"To be honest, Cyrus, the pain's quite bad. I'm sure it'll ease off, but just now my whole body's throbbing like I've got a drum inside me."

No one replied. They all knew, as Zavar himself did, that wounds like his took weeks to heal, if they healed at all. Even innocent-looking cuts became infected and the sufferer died of blood poisoning. And Zavar's wound did not look innocent.

Cyrus searched his mind for a solution. He had been on many Tallin salvage parties bringing back medical supplies from shops and other buildings that had escaped looting. Sadly, they didn't know how to use the loot properly and powerful drugs, well passed their use-by date, often made patients sicker rather than better. Did the literate Yonners know better?

"You know how to read, Roxanne," he said slowly, "and where you were brought up they have books –"

"Only three, Cyrus."

"Yes, but don't those books tell you about healing, about cures and that sort of thing? Like in the time of the Long Dead. Maybe you know something to help Zavar."

Roxanne shook her head and, despite the cruel circumstances, smiled at his optimism. Not for the first time in her presence, Cyrus felt a wave of unexplained happiness wash over him.

"I wish I could be of use," she said, looking round at the others. "Unfortunately, the Books of Yonne don't speak much of science or healing. They are, well, odd. Difficult to understand – not the words themselves but the information and ideas they stand for. Generations of Yonner scholars have argued over them, trying to work out what they mean."

Before anyone asked what these books were, the sound of barking began again in the distance. "Come on!" called Cyrus, snapping back into his role as leader. "I'm sure Zavar will be OK – and Roxanne can tell us about her weird books later. So, let's go! If the mission gets through, there'll be more books and knowledge than we ever dreamed of. But if we fail…" He left the sentence unfinished.

Cyrus and Taja helped Zavar to his feet and the party continued on its way. Out in front, after Roxanne and Navid had walked in silence for a while, she turned to him and asked earnestly, "You know how to keep wounds clean, don't you Navid?"

"Yeah. That's why you put those leaves on Zavar's shoulder. Keep out the dirt."

"Yes, but it needs to be properly cleaned. Water, Navid. We need to find water to wash the wound. Have you ever been here before, on a patrol?"

Navid shook his head. "Never. But if it's water you want, I know a fellow who'll find it for you." He stooped down and patted Corby's massive flank. "Drink time, old boy," he whispered. "Go on! Drink! Find drink!"

The dog looked up at him as if to say, "Water? Well, why didn't you say so earlier?" then raised his nose in the air and sniffed. Seconds later, he was bundling off to the right, leaving the Tallins struggling to keep up. After a good deal of sniffing and snuffling, and a quick diversion in pursuit of a startled rabbit, Corby found what he was looking for. Galloping ahead of his master, he plunged into a shallow ravine and was soon lapping happily at the sluggish brown stream that ran along the bottom.

Though the water was not as clean as they would have wished and tasted of mud, it had to do. After they had drunk their fill and replenished their water bottles – some of leather, others battered relics rescued from a Long Dead store – Taja insisted that it was she who bathed Zavar's wound and bandaged fresh leaves to his gashed flesh. She frowned as she worked but when Roxanne asked if she needed any help, she dismissed the offer with a curt, "No! I can manage on my own."

Meanwhile, Cyrus and Navid discussed their next move. The stream was a triple blessing. Its water was essential for drinking and washing – and as a means of evading the Zeds. If they waded along it for a thousand paces or more, Cyrus reckoned, there was no way the dogs would be able to follow their scent.

Slipping on wet rocks and ducking beneath overhanging branches, the party scrambled along the bed of the stream before striking out again across country. As darkness fell, they reached a clump of stumpy trees whose swollen trunks rose like the ruins of a vast temple against the glowing embers of the sky. There, thoroughly exhausted by the events of the day, they collapsed to the ground and slept.

Taja woke first. Lying next to Cyrus, she put out her hand and gently shook his shoulder. He yawned and opened his eyes. "Shh!" she whispered, placing a finger to her lips and rolling over so that he felt her breath on his cheek. "Listen, Cyrus. We must talk."

"Yes?" He was very conscious of Taja's lips hovering near his and of her hand still resting against his shoulder.

"You know what I think of Roxanne…"

Cyrus sighed. "Yes, you've made it pretty obvious. But you've seen how she behaves, her reactions to the Zeds…" He glanced across to where Roxanne lay. She was still asleep, her head pillowed on her hands. "She's honest, Taja. I know she is."

Taja came still closer. "Alright, I agree she's terrified of the Zeds. Maybe that's why she's acting for them? Odd, wasn't it, that they knew where and when to ambush us? And in the fight, did any of them go for her seriously, even try to injure her? Think about it, Cyrus," she added slowly, her lips brushing against his. "Think about it."

"I will. Of course I will." Despite her clouded motives, he recognized the logic behind what she was saying.

"And while you're thinking…" Her mouth closed over his.

Cyrus turned away. "No, Taja. Not now, not here." What he meant was not her. If there was any time for kissing on this mission, he hoped it might be with someone else.

As soon as it was light, the party rose, ate a little of the bread they had brought with them, and set off again. Urged on by Cyrus, they moved as quickly as Zavar could manage through the heat of the day, walking for a few thousand paces, resting, then moving on again. Where possible they followed the route of ancient roads, but keeping a few hundred paces to the side of the main track for fear of attracting Zeds. For the same reason, they hugged the shadows, avoiding skylines and open spaces.

Cyrus had plenty of time to think about Taja's remarks. He was sure she was wrong, but throughout the day he watched Roxanne carefully to see whether she was leaving any sort of trail for the pursuing Zeds. He saw nothing.

On the third morning, still pondering Taja's accusations and looking for an opportunity to get to know Roxanne better, Cyrus fell in beside her and started chatting. Timur and his tribe, he suggested, may well have given up the chase when they lost track of their prey in the stream. Roxanne simply shook her head and said she wished she were so optimistic. Seeing the pain on her face that the subject caused, Cyrus switched to less troubling matters. Life in Yonne, he asked, how was it different from that in Della Tallis?

Roxanne relaxed and spoke eagerly of her past, her upbringing and her children. As Cyrus listened, enthralled by her wit and charm as much as by what she said, he wondered how he could ever have doubted her integrity. After a while, the conversation came round to the Books of Yonne. He had never seen a book, he reminded her, and wanted to know what they looked like and what they meant.

Roxanne laughed as she described how different the three she had read were: one fat and shiny, all bright colours and pictures; another looked dull, though it had very intelligent words inside; and the third – well, the third was the really strange one.

"How strange?" asked Cyrus.

64

"We don't know why it was written. The author –"

"What's that?"

"Author? Oh, that's a person who writes a book. They set out the words on paper. We think there were several ways of doing this, some by hand, others by machine."

Cyrus was lost. "OK, you can explain that later. But why's this book so odd?"

"It's a story about children living in the time of the Long Dead. One of them doesn't want to get older. You know how the Long Dead grew older slowly and lived for many, many more years than we do?'

"Years being our winters – of course, yes."

"Well, this boy doesn't want to grow up. He's afraid, like we are of our Death Month. Some Yonne scholars said the man who wrote it – James – knew that the Great Death was going to happen. He saw that one day there would be only young people – young to the Long Dead way of thinking, that is."

"Sounds really weird!" muttered Cyrus.

"That's not all. In this story, people fly through the sky."

"Is it real? I mean, was it actually like that in the time of the Long Dead?"

"We don't know. Maybe this was just a dream…"

"This book, does it have a name?"

"Yes. It's called *Peter Pan*."

"Peter Pan, Peter Pan," repeated Cyrus to himself. "Roxanne, could you show me how to write that?"

"Of course."

"I was thinking. If anything happened…Well, it would be

good if two of us knew how to read, wouldn't it?"

They were interrupted by a cry from Navid. He was pointing towards the ruins of a town in the valley below.

Constants normally avoided such places. There was something deeply sad about their rows of crumbling, ivy-clad buildings, fallen wires and the rusting shells of vehicles. The stench of decay lingered like poisonous pollen in the heavy air. Having once feasted on human flesh, the armies of sharp-toothed rats that lived there were bold and aggressive. Birds of prey circled silently overhead, snakes eased themselves between cracks in the hot concrete, and wild dogs lay in the sun, licking their flyblown sores. No Constant, however brave, ever felt comfortable in the towns of their ancestors, for all their faded glory.

Nevertheless, patrols did occasionally venture into the barren and overgrown streets in search of materials that might be useful. Metal was most highly prized, followed by ceramics. Navid had been on a couple of these salvage operations and he wondered whether they might go into this town to look for bandages and medicines for Zavar. Roxanne would be able to read the writing on any packets or bottles they came across.

Taja put a stop to the idea. "I'm the only Mudir on this mission," she said briskly, "so I'll make this decision. We'll press on."

Navid looked puzzled. "Er, I thought Cyrus was the leader?" he said.

"That was before I arrived. Now it's different, Navid."

Cyrus didn't like the way the conversation was going.

Divisions and squabbles over leadership were the last thing they wanted. "Look," he said firmly, "this will get us nowhere. Out here there are no Emirs or Mudirs or anything. We're all in it together. I'll take charge when it comes to fighting, and all other decisions we'll make together, OK?"

Taking the silence that followed as agreement, he asked Zavar whether he wanted them to go to look for medicine. The wounded swordsman shook his head. It would be far too risky for a few of them to enter a town and they should press on, he said. Time was precious and his condition did not seem to be deteriorating. Although his fractured shoulder was still extremely painful, the wound was no longer hurting so badly.

Appearances can be cruelly deceptive. In the middle of the afternoon, as they were climbing a rocky slope to avoid passing through a ravine, Zavar collapsed.

He staggered forward, cutting open his cheek on a flint, and lay face down, breathing heavily. Taja came up and knelt beside him. "Fever," she announced, laying a hand on his forehead. "He is very sick."

Cyrus and Navid turned their friend over and made him as comfortable as they could on the hard ground. Roxanne gave him a drink and carefully untied the bandage on his shoulder. When the leaves were removed, the nauseating stench was overpowering. The wound had become badly infected. To the width of two hands, the flesh around it was red and swollen. Yellow puss oozed from the jagged scar and from the sunset flush on Zavar's face it was clear that his body temperature had risen alarmingly. Beneath the skin, his flesh was starting to rot.

Leaving Roxanne with the injured man, the Tallins moved away to discuss what to do. The predicament was new to them. Back home an ill or injured person was taken to the Sick House, and when they died – the usual outcome – their body was burned on the Ash Pile. There was little room for sentiment because the passing of friends and acquaintances was a common occurrence. In a world where everyone who had seen eighteen winters knew to within a few days when their life would end, the arrival of that moment might be sad but it was hardly a surprise.

That did not mean they were willing simply to abandon Zavar to a wretched fate. Apart from rare executions and war killing – an ugly necessity to prevent even greater slaughter – Constants still prized life, with its bittersweet mix of joys and sorrows. As their proverb said, what else was there? Besides, Cyrus asked, wasn't their mission itself about the preciousness of life, a quest for the secrets of those who had once enjoyed it in abundance?

"Maybe," said Taja, shrugging her shoulders in a matter-of-fact manner. "But Zavar will die soon. So what's to be done? The nearest Sick House is back in Della Tallis."

Cyrus looked at her. She was right, of course, but did she have to be that blunt? "It's our duty to look after him," he reminded her, "whatever the circumstances."

"That's a Tallin rule," replied Taja quickly. "As you have never stopped telling us, things are different out here. What do you think, Navid?"

"Er, well, I suppose you're both right. In a way." Where possible, Navid avoided abstract questions of right and wrong.

He was more comfortable doing what he felt was correct. His instinct for natural justice rarely failed.

"So, Taja proposes we leave him here and press on," Cyrus announced. "Any other ideas?"

He was playing for time, trying to make up his own mind. Zavar might take days to die. During that time, Roxanne's life would also be ebbing towards its close and Timur's dogs might pick up their scent and resume the chase. Once again, he faced the heart-breaking clash of upbringing and instinct.

The discussion was interrupted by Zavar calling to them. The water had revived him, he said, and his fever had subsided a little. With his head in Roxanne's lap, he looked up at his friends with bloodshot eyes. "Listen," he rasped, "I know what's going on. This is the end for me. I didn't get very far, did I?"

"You saved Taja's life in the fight," said Navid.

"Maybe, maybe. But now I'm just a boulder tied to your legs."

"Nonsense!" said Cyrus, trying to sound reassuring. "You'll be better soon, Zavar. It takes more than a dead-brained Zed to put you down!"

Zavar's cracked lips parted in a smile. "Come on, Cyrus! Don't fool yourself. We're Constants, remember? We're honest, true to the old ways. So if this Soterion thing can bring them back, then nothing, absolutely nothing must get in the way of our finding it."

Raising his right arm, he clasped his friend tightly by the ankle. "Please, Cyrus. This is my last wish. I am a burden. Leave me, and the four of you continue the mission. I beg you."

4
The Children of Gova

Timur's annoyance, having swollen to angry frustration, was now close to fury. He did not take kindly to being thwarted by anyone, let alone by a woman who had humiliated him.

Sitting in the shade of a myrtle tree to prevent the midday sun burning his oyster-white skin, the chief of the Grozny Zeds ordered a further six of his personal bodyguard to join the search. Before him slipped the sluggish brown brook into which, two days earlier, the Tallins had waded to throw the pursuing hounds off the scent. Somewhere, upstream or downstream, left or right, he knew his enemies must have climbed the bank and continued their journey. The hunt had been going on for almost two days now, and still there were no clues.

Timur had set off in pursuit of the mission shortly after hearing of the failure of the ambush. First, though, he had watched the execution by impalement of the three men – one of whom was already dying of his injuries – who had brought him the news of the defeat and of their failure to detain Roxanne.

"What can I do?" he had explained to them with a mirthless grin. "I would have to kill you for disobedience if you hadn't told me of your defeat, and now you have to die for the disgrace of losing a battle. What a pity! No choice. Death or…death!"

The three prisoners stared open-mouthed as they struggled to understand the sadistic logic. Like all common Zeds, they were virtually incapable of reasoning. But Sheza, the chief's nominated successor, was learning to think and act differently. Standing beside his master, he found the whole situation immensely amusing. "Clever Timur!" he chuckled, pointing at the doomed culprits. "Die in the fight – or die on the spit! Ha, ha, ha!"

The Malik looked at him with a mixture of contempt and approval. "Good lad, Sheza! You're getting there." Nevertheless, he made a mental note to arrange for his heir to receive further education from the next intelligent Constant they captured. The young man still thought in the manner of a commoner, he realised with a sigh, which was barely thinking at all. Unless he showed a marked improvement, he'd never make a Malik of the Grozny.

Timur stared into the muddy water. The longer this went on, the more serious it became. He had lost six valuable hunting dogs to Tallin arrows in trying to recapture that Roxanne woman, and the failed ambush had cost him twenty men. Tribe numbers had been falling recently and he really ought to be raiding Constant settlements or other Zed tribes to stock up on breeding slaves. Of the thirty-five or so female prisoners in the Grozny encampment, only half were pregnant. That was something else he needed to attend to, personally if he had the time.

For the moment, he had to get after those infuriating Tallins and the Yonner they were protecting. If he could find their trail again and see which direction they were headed in…

"Malik! Malik!" An urgent voice interrupted Timur's musings. He looked up to see a man of around thirteen winters running along the edge of the stream towards him. Reaching the point where his chief was seated, the near-naked youth scrambled up the bank and fell on his knees before him.

"Yes, Giv? Speak!"

"Dog sniff good! Good sniff! Find!" Giv panted, looking up with eyes that were half delighted, half anxious. No Grozny ever knew how their Malik was going to react – that was part of his mystique and his power.

Timur raised a pale eyebrow. "Are you trying to say that a dog has found the scent of the people we're hunting, Giv?"

The youth nodded vigorously. "Yeah! Yeah! Good scent!"

"Where?"

"There!" Giv waved an arm in the general area of the stream.

"Yes, dungbrain, but which side of the stream is the trail?"

"Side, Malik?"

"Yes, side of the stream, ratspittle. Left or right?"

Giv, beyond the limit of his vocabulary, gawped helplessly. "Eh? Lefrite?"

Struggling to control his frustration, the chief told the messenger to stand in the middle of the stream and indicate which way the dog had moved off. It was left – his quarry was still following the noonday sun.

Timur rose and began pacing up and down in the mottled shadows like a ghost. Sheza and the bodyguard behind him watched in awe and admiration: Malik Timur did more thinking in an afternoon than all of them together managed in a whole moon. Except perhaps for Jamshid and Jumshid, the bodyguard captains.

At some point, Timur realised, the Tallins would have to cross the river which the Zeds bluntly called 'No-Man' – no man who entered the broad stream swarming with crocodiles and poisonous water snakes was ever seen again. The only way across was by the one remaining Long Dead bridge, a rusty and dilapidated structure whose central pier had been carried away by floods long ago. Careful travellers could still get to the other bank by balancing precariously for about ten paces along the two corroded steel rails remaining over the void.

At the bridge, Timur planned to cut off his quarry, seize the woman and kill her escort. But how to get there before his prey, which was now at least two days ahead of him?

"Jumshid!"

A squat man of seventeen winters but many fewer teeth lumbered forward from the ranks of the bodyguard. "Malik?"

"The three horses we seized in the rainy season – what condition are they in now?"

"Condition?" repeated the captain. Although more fluent than Giv, many of his master's words remained a mystery to him.

"Yes, condition, loghead! How – are – they? Can they be ridden?"

"Ah! One is sick and will die soon, Malik. The men want to eat it."

"Well, they can't! And the other two?"

"The big one is good for riding. The small one is limping – only light man can ride."

"That will do, Jumshid," said Timur, his pallid hands twitching with nervous excitement. "You take the bigger one and Sheza the smaller one, and ride to No-Man River. You know the way?"

"Yes, Malik!"

"Good. When you are there, go to the bridge. Bridge. Do you understand?"

Jumshid hesitated. "Old iron over No-Man, Malik?"

"That's it." Timur, who was a tall man, walked up to the captain until he towered above him like a gigantic stalk. "Now, do whatever is necessary to stop the Tallins crossing the bridge. Break the bridge down. Repeat!"

"Break the bridge down."

"Or stand on the other side and shoot anyone trying to cross. Repeat!"

"Shoot anyone trying to cross," echoed Jumshid faithfully. He prided himself on being one of the best of all the Grozny at remembering orders.

"Excellent. Hold the Tallins there and we will charge up behind them and destroy them. Simple, eh?"

"Charge up behind and destroy! Simple!"

Timur clamped a hand on his captain's shoulder and ordered him to leave with Sheza immediately. When they had gone, the Malik looked up at the canopy of leaves above him and paused. It was true that if those Tallins followed the sun they would arrive at the river, but on the way they might meet with something else. Yes, on the same route lay the settlement of the Constants who called themselves the Children of Gova. Well, if the Tallins met with them, anything might happen...

The Malik shook his head. No, the chances of them bumping into the Gova settlement were remote. It was too small and isolated. The river was where he and his men would make for, and fast. There he would take his revenge, making the elusive Roxanne regret with every fibre of her bewitching body the moment she had outwitted him.

All this time, unsure whether or not he was allowed to move, the youth who had brought the news of the rediscovered trail was still standing in the middle of the stream. Timur stared at him for half a second, before he remembered who he was and said, "Ah, yes! Still with us, Giv? Tell the men to stop the search and come here."

"Stop search? Yes, Malik!" The youth began to wade off downstream.

"And Giv, I am pleased with you," Timur shouted after him. A grin spread across the young man's face. "I will give you a prize. Tonight you may play with the breeding slaves."

Grinning like a new moon and muttering "Prize! Prize!" over and over to himself, Giv splashed off round a bend in the stream. What a useful double order, thought Timur. With a single command I've rewarded loyalty and done something about the numbers problem. I must try that again some time.

Ahead of Timur and his tribe, Taja was also issuing commands. "Before anyone responds to Zavar's request," she began, looking straight at Cyrus and then down at the wounded man himself, "I feel it's my duty to make our position clear."

"Here we go again," muttered Navid in a half whisper.

Taja spun round to confront him. "Shut up, Navid! It's high time we got this straight. I am risking – probably sacrificing – my life for a very dubious mission. All of us are. We're in the middle of nowhere, surrounded by hostile Zeds and almost certainly being followed by the Grozny, the most dangerous of them all. We can't tell for sure whether Roxanne is one of us, a Constant, or whether she is telling us the truth with her Soterion story. She doesn't even seem to know where we're going! And has it ever occurred to you that she may herself have been tricked?"

Eyes flaming, Taja paused and looked round the group. Though the Tallins knew she could be fierce, this was beyond anything they had seen previously and Cyrus decided it was best to let her have her say. He was impressed, sure, but watching her face closely, did he notice a hint of fear behind those flashing eyes?

"If I say no more quarrelling," she ordered, "that's what happens. Got that into your heads? We're Constants. Or at least we say we are." She looked scornfully towards Roxanne. "And Constants are true to the ideas of the Long Dead: courage, respect and unity. If we lose those, we are nothing. Mere Zeds!" Again she looked hard at Roxanne.

"Zavar, as he has told us himself, is dying. He has asked

us to leave him here and continue the mission. He has shown courage. Now it's up to us to match it with respect and unity. That's what I demand we do."

Cyrus looked across at Roxanne. There was no point in trying to argue, ran the unspoken message between them. It would only make things worse.

Navid was less of a politician. Before Cyrus could stop him, he shook his shaggy head in anger and reminded Taja what they had all agreed: although she was a Mudir back home, out here she was just one of them. He had joined the mission because Cyrus was leading it, not her. She had not been invited. If she didn't like it, why didn't she go home and do her bossing there?

The situation was getting out of control. When Zavar and Cyrus both tried to speak at the same time, Navid folded his arms and turned his back on all of them. Taja stood breathing noisily, staring at the long hair curling over Navid's shoulders. To their left, a startled bird screeched into the hot, dry sky.

It was Roxanne who calmed things down. Walking quietly over to Navid, she laid a hand on his shoulder.

"Get off, Taj –" he began, turning round sharply. He stopped, confused. "Oh, sorry, Roxanne. I didn't realise it was you."

"Don't worry, Navid," she replied. "No need to apologise." She spoke so calmly and clearly that it was hard to believe she had heard all the harsh insinuations of Taja's rant. "Since I seem to be the cause of all this trouble, please let me say something."

"Why not? Please go on." Taja made no effort to hide her scorn.

In a manner that was close to motherly, Roxanne kept a hand

on Navid's arm. Her voice, as when she spoke before the Majlis back in Della Tallis, was unquestionably sincere.

"You are all, every one of you, brave and wonderful people. I know what you have sacrificed and I hope that one day, when our mission is accomplished, you will be recognised as the saviours of our people.

"I have not lied to you and I will not lie to you. My story is true. I believe there is a Soterion and that we will find it and reveal its secrets. But we can do this only if we pull together. Please."

Navid nodded his head slightly. "As for our poor friend Zavar," Roxanne concluded, "his fate is not for us to decide, is it? He had made his decision and, Cyrus and Navid, I believe we would do him a great dishonour if we ignored it. Do you want him to die knowing he may be the cause of his friends' deaths, too?"

"No, thank you!" cut in Zavar in a manner that brought a smile to every face.

The crisis was over. At Cyrus' insistence they all shook hands and set about making the dying man as comfortable as possible. Navid and Cyrus erected a shelter from branches to protect him from the sun. While Roxanne settled him within this leafy tent, Taja went off to pick some medicinal herbs she had seen growing nearby. She knew a bit about plants, she announced when she returned, and these would help Zavar sleep if the pain became too great. Cyrus was tempted to ask about the leaves she had placed on Zavar's wound at the stream: if she knew what she was doing, why had her treatment failed to prevent the infection spreading? In the end he thought better of it, deciding the wound must have been inflicted by a poisoned weapon. Besides, there had been enough confrontation for one day.

They finally departed as the afternoon was drawing to a close, walking fast as if they wanted to get away not just from Zavar but also from their decision to leave him. For a long time no one spoke.

Finally, as the disc of the dying sun dipped beneath the tops of the tallest trees, Cyrus became aware of someone coming up behind him. It was Roxanne.

"Cyrus, why do you think she joined us?" Her voice was different: quicker, more urgent.

The question took him by surprise. "You mean Taj –"

"Yes. Come on, let's stop pretending, Cyrus. We haven't known each other long, but I think we can trust each other, can't we?"

"Of course." With the smile of recognition that passed between them, he again felt that thrill of delight at just being with her. It was a wonderful emotion, yet painfully confusing when death sat poised visibly on every shoulder.

"So, why's she here?" Roxanne asked again.

"Tricky. Part of it is that, well, she and I were lovers. Sort of."

"Were, Cyrus?"

"Yes, were. Nothing serious. She was keener than me – made the relationship a bit lopsided. One day Leiss told me, in confidence, I was 'unwise' – that was the word he used – to tangle with Taja. But she was attractive in a dangerous sort of way. I admired her sharp mind, her cleverness, her skill at seeing what mattered and what didn't."

"Understandable."

"Yes, but it wasn't exactly a romantic relationship and I probably shouldn't have got so involved. I felt guilty sometimes – I suppose I was also a bit sorry for her, reaching her Death Year not having had any children."

Roxanne shook her head. "From what I've seen, Cyrus, and I don't want to be unkind, but is she the sort of woman who needs your pity – or anyone else's?"

He laughed. "You're right. She's as tough as they come. Ambitious, too: Taja does what's good for Taja. Honestly, I could never figure out what she saw in me."

"You couldn't?" Roxanne's voice was lighter, teasing. "Then I'll tell you. She saw the future, Cyrus. She saw a tall, well-built and handsome man, more than a winter younger than herself, who was both a warrior and a thinker. A true leader. Someone with a body and a mind – and a heart."

Cyrus tutted and shook his head.

"Don't recognise yourself, Cyrus?"

"No. I'm no leader. I'm too full of questions I can't answer."

"That's what makes you different. Most people don't even ask the questions." Again they exchanged glances, confirming with their eyes the cocktail of physical and mental attraction growing between them.

"You're different, too, Roxanne. You know that, don't you?"

She shrugged and flashed him a quick smile. "Maybe."

"Unlike anyone I've ever met."

They walked on in silence for a few moments, each taking in

the significance of what had been said.

"But we must be careful, Roxanne," continued Cyrus, lowering his voice. "Very careful. She can be ruthless, you know."

"I'm sure."

"Going back to why she's here. Well, it may be partly because of me, but it's also because I reckon she's changed her mind about you. To begin with, back in the Majlis, I'm certain she really was afraid you were a spy, a traitor. Now I'm sure she knows in her heart of hearts – but won't admit it – that you've been telling the truth about the Soterion all along. That's why she's here and why she keeps telling us she's a Mudir. She was furious when she wasn't chosen to be our Emir – this gives her a chance to be something even more important."

"Leader of the Soterion Mission?"

"Yes. She wants us to succeed. That's why you're safe – for the moment."

Roxanne thought for a moment. "You mean she'll put up with me as long as I'm the only one who can read? A bit nasty, but I see what you mean. I thought it was odd when she approved of me teaching you. Once you know how…"

"Exactly. But we're not there yet, are we? I only know the 'P' for 'Peter Pan'!"

"Then it's time for another lesson, Cy! You don't mind if I call you 'Cy', do you? Just between ourselves."

"No, not if you let me call you 'Roxy'."

She hesitated. "Someone used to call me that. They're no longer alive."

"I'm sorry. I'll stick to 'Roxanne'. It's a lovely name."

"No, it's alright. Call me Roxy. It'll make me feel young again." After a brief pause, she went on briskly, "OK, let's begin with the first letter of the alphabet. It's 'A', as in 'IKE - A'."

"Hang on, Roxy! What's an 'IKEA'?"

"Ah! It's found in the second of the three Books of Yonne. Its name is the *IKEA Catalogue*."

The travellers had been climbing steadily since leaving Della Tallis and in the hills, although the days were still blisteringly hot, at night the temperature dropped sharply. Afraid to light a fire in case it attracted the Zeds, they slept close to each other for warmth.

On the first two nights, Taja had made sure she was next to Cyrus. When they lay down at the end of the third day, however, she placed herself beside Navid and whispered to him for some time before they fell asleep.

Cyrus nudged Roxanne and pointed towards his friend. "Eh?" he mouthed.

"Wants an ally," she mouthed back. Then, leaning across and putting her mouth to his ear, she whispered, "Trying to get between you and Navid?"

Cyrus rolled over and gently pushed back her hair. By starlight the curve of her neck was as smooth as glass. "Impossible!" he replied, brushing her ear with his lips as he spoke.

She smiled and felt for his hand. Not long afterwards, still holding on to each other, they fell asleep.

By the morning of the fourth day, the mission had eaten nearly all the food they had brought with them from Della Tallis. At lower altitude, there were plenty of wild fruits and berries; now the land was less fertile and the vegetation thinner. Taja's skill as an archer meant they did not go hungry: she bagged a couple of plump rabbits that they skinned and roasted over an open fire lit with Cyrus' flint and steel. Although the meat was nourishing and tasted good, the process took time and there was always a danger that the smoke would be seen by prowling Zeds.

Corby had no such worries. He loved being in the open all day long, optimistically chasing birds, growling at snakes from a safe distance, and munching happily on the many bones he found lying about in the increasingly bleak landscape. He didn't realise it, of course, but it was this bone-hunting that brought about a sudden and dramatic change in the group's fortunes.

Around mid-morning on the fourth day of the mission, Corby came bounding up to Navid with his latest snack firmly between his teeth. His master glanced at him and smiled. "Good boy, Corby! Got yourself a nice something to chew on, have you?"

Navid stopped and looked at the bone again. Hang on a bit! That wasn't from a wolf or even a deer. It looked more like…He called the others to take a look. Yes, there was no mistaking it. The dog was gnawing away at human thighbone.

"Where'd you find it, Corby?" Navid asked, pointing at the bone. For once, the dog did not understand. Navid tried again. "Same!" he cried. "Go find! Bone!"

Corby looked at him as if wondering whether he should

reveal the whereabouts of his secret larder, then set off across the rocky ground to their right. Keeping a wary eye open for danger, Navid followed.

Soon afterwards, the rest of the party heard him shouting. "Hey, Cy! Taja! Roxanne! Come and look at this! Quick! It's amazing!"

Navid was standing next to Corby on the rim of a small and shallow canyon, staring down into it. When the others joined him, they gasped in astonishment. Below, less than five hundred paces away, single-storey huts were ranged round a large hall. Nearby, glinting in the sunlight, was what looked like a gigantic mirror. All around, right across the floor of the canyon, stretched neat, bright green gardens in which men and women were working. Near the hall, children were playing, their shrill cries carrying easily up to where the mission stood in open-mouthed amazement.

"It's sort of…sort of how they say things were before the Great Death!" gasped Navid. "Like we're looking at a little dream world. There aren't any guards, either. I don't understand. Why haven't the Zeds got them?"

Cyrus' gaze moved from the huts and the garden to where the greenery suddenly ended. The abrupt boundary was marked by a wire fence as tall as two men, and the ground immediately beyond it was piled high with hundreds of human skeletons. Half a dozen bodies were sprawled across the bones. The corpses mummified rapidly in the dry heat, and two of these grizzled remains, which had lain there about a month or so, retained a layer of dried skin. It was from the leg of one of these that Corby had stolen his macabre breakfast.

"Skeletons," said Cyrus, speaking more to himself than to the others. "Human skeletons. Dozens and dozens, and they're…"

"All Zeds!" finished Taja with unusual enthusiasm. "At least, some of them are. Look at that one there, on top of the heap," she cried, pointing eagerly. "It still has flesh on it, and the one next to it – you can see the tattoo from here!"

Roxanne frowned and instinctively traced with her forefinger the ugly Z-shaped scar on her forehead.

"Well, I suggest we go down there and find out what's going on," said Cyrus. "It looks safe enough. They're obviously Constants of some sort or else they wouldn't be farming and living in huts and so on. And I wonder what killed those Zeds? It might be disease, so we'd better be careful."

Roxanne's mind was racing. She ought to know the answer to Cyrus' question. There were clues, lots of them, in the *IKEA Catalogue* that she had spent many days studying. Her thoughts kept returning to the expression "fatal shock", but on each occasion she rejected it as an absurd impossibility. Key information was missing.

Eager to find out more about the strange settlement and its bizarre boundary of dead Zeds, they agreed to go and investigate. Cyrus, closely followed by the other three, set off eagerly after Corby down the stony slope into the ravine. At the bottom, Roxanne swept her hair forward to cover her scar and they cautiously approached what appeared to be a gate. It was made from the same shining steel wire as the rest of the fence, though the space before it was clear of bones.

By now their arrival had been noticed by people within the settlement, and a small crowd gathered to watch as the mission made its way towards the entrance. When they were perhaps a dozen paces from the wire, a tall man with a surprisingly full beard and wearing what looked like a white toga stepped forward and raised both hands in the air in a dramatic fashion.

"Halt!" he cried. "What strangers are they who seek to enter the domain of the Children of Gova?"

"Eh?" grunted Navid. "What's he on about?"

Roxanne smiled. "Shh! He's only asking who we are."

Cyrus advanced a few steps. "We are Constants from the communities of Della Tallis and Yonne," he called clearly. "We come in peace seeking shelter and food."

On the other side of the fence, the robed man consulted with those around him before coming forward again and announcing, "Travellers, you are indeed welcome. In the name of Gova, permit them to enter!"

A man and a woman immediately ran out and, with great care, grasped hold of the worn plastic handles that operated the gates. Roxanne watched, fascinated. Metal fence, plastic handles…There was a word lurking at the back of her mind, a word that would explain everything.

The gates creaked loudly as they swung back. To judge by the noise, thought Roxanne, they hadn't been opened for some time.

"Once more, welcome!" cried the man in the white robe. "Enter this holy place!" As Cyrus warily led the way through the entrance, the speaker issued a bizarre warning. "Beware, guests!

Touch not the fence for fear of angering the Mighty Gova!"

Cyrus was level with the wire when Roxanne suddenly remembered the missing word. "Insulated" – that was it. The exact phrase from the *IKEA Catalogue* was "Double insulated to protect against the risk of fatal electric shock."

Yonne scholars had worked out from the *Catalogue* and from the many ruins scattered across the countryside that their ancestors used a force known as "electricity". Travelling through metal, it was both powerful and deadly…Roxanne looked again at the steel wires of the fence and at the bones and bodies piled outside it. What had the man said? Touch not the fence…

Impossible! These people were not Long Dead, so they couldn't have electricity. She didn't understand…Something was wrong. The place didn't feel right.

"Cyrus!" she called urgently. "Cyrus, I'm not sure – "

The man in the toga cut her short. "Enter please, stranger. The gates are closing now. Hurry!" His voice sounded harsher, less welcoming.

The other three, well ahead of her, were already inside. She had no choice. If she remained alone in the wilderness, she would perish in no time. Quickening her step, she hurried through the gates and heard them shut with a reverberating clang behind her.

The visitors found themselves on an earth roadway that led to the hall they had seen from the edge of the ravine. Before them, dressed in identical yellow robes, stood twelve men adorned with a variety of beards, some more successful than others. All were of seventeen or eighteen winters. The white-clad figure who had invited the Constants in – obviously their leader – stepped forward once more.

"How honoured are we that you are come amongst us," he chanted in a weird sing-song voice. "My name is Ozlam, the High Father. As Children of Gova, it is our duty and pleasure to feed and care for you. We ask little in return."

Cyrus was starting to feel distinctly uncomfortable. "Thank you, Ozlam," he replied. "We are grateful to you for your hospitality, but we don't want much. Just a little food and some water, and we'll be on our way again. We have a vital mission to fulfil."

"A mission? How noble!" interrupted Ozlam. "However, now you are within this glorious precinct, we first require you to follow a hallowed rule of the Children of Gova."

"Rule?" queried Taja. She too was wondering whether entering this bizarre settlement had been such a good idea. "What rule is that?"

"Such a sweet and simple regulation," chanted Ozlam, casting a bony smile over each of the new arrivals in turn. "All visitors who enter this most sacred place must surrender their weapons to be destroyed."

5
Heresy!

It took Sheza and Captain Jumshid almost three days to ride to the River No-Man. It need not have taken that long, but the two were sworn rivals: whenever they came to a stretch of level and open countryside, they insisted on racing each other across it. Sheza, the younger and lighter man, won the first race easily. He got his victory, however, by mercilessly whipping his lame horse until its sides ran with blood.

By noon of the second day, the wretched creature was able to take no more. With a tragic whinny of despair, it crumpled to the ground, flinging Sheza headlong into the dust.

For a few moments, he lay stunned. Then gradually, as he realised what had happened, he was consumed by rage. Never, in all his thirteen winters of life, had he been so humiliated. Eyes blazing, he picked himself up and walked over to where his horse lay, quivering with exhaustion.

"Traitor!" he screamed, kicking the blood- and foam-flecked flanks of the poor beast. He had only just learned the word and was keen to show it off before Jumshid. "Traitor! Traitor! Traitor!" he cried again and again, his foot thumping heavily with each frenzied repetition. "The one who will be Malik needs honour, not scorn. Animal!"

Jumshid looked down from his saddle and grinned. "Ha! Captain Jumshid win race!" he rumbled, revealing teeth like tree stumps in a tropical swamp. "I win, Sheza!" So foul was his breath that even the flies retreated from his open mouth. "Jumshid win! Ha! Ha!"

"Silence, ratvomit!" yelled his furious companion, copying one of Timur's favourite expressions. "I will tell the Malik!"

At the mention of Timur, a flash of fear slid across Jumshid's battered face and he stopped his mockery. That was not enough for Sheza. As there was now only one horse, he declared, he would ride it. The Captain could walk.

"Walk?" challenged Jumshid. "I have horse and I am on horse! You walk!"

Fearing that his partner might ride away and leave him to fend for himself in this bleak place, Sheza urged his lazy brain to come up with a solution. "If I walk," he said with careful menace, "you will have to go slow and we may get to the River No-Man after Constants. Bad for me – and you."

Jumshid frowned and said nothing.

"Listen – I have a clever idea. You and me ride the same horse! Then the Malik will be all smiles for us!"

The prospect of a smiling Timur – something he had rarely, if ever, witnessed – was more than enough to win Jumshid over. Leaving his own mount to die in the barren wilderness, Sheza swung himself up behind the captain and the pair trotted off in the direction of the river.

Perhaps Jumshid's horse had lost heart on witnessing the fate of its partner? Perhaps two men were too heavy a burden for its exhausted and underfed frame? Whatever the reason, it kept going for only a few thousand paces before it too collapsed and died. Obliged to finish their journey on foot, the Zeds were in a foul temper when they reached the river. Their mood was hardly improved when, standing a safe distance from the water's edge, they saw not a pillar, not a girder of the bridge they had been sent to destroy.

Jumshid scratched at his lice-ridden head. "Where it vanish? Someone do our job, Sheza. Bridge gone."

Now shut inside the fenced community of the Children of Gova, Cyrus was almost as confused as Jumshid. Being asked to surrender their weapons for destruction was an impossible request! Trying not to show his anxiety, he took a step towards the bearded man who called himself High Father of the settlement.

"Ozlam – my name's Cyrus, by the way – we're grateful to you for your kindness," he began, "but we'll need our weapons to continue our mission. We'll give them to you, if you insist, only if they're returned when we leave."

Ozlam did not reply immediately. Rather, he again let his eyes travel over the faces of the new arrivals standing in front of him. Cyrus recognised the look: he was assessing them, astutely, one by one.

"Dear travellers," he said, speaking in his measured,

sing-song voice, "the Children of Gova live in peace. We have no weapons. We have no need of weapons. We do not like weapons. Gova, the Great Gova whose power lies in the fence, is our shield and defender. We need no other.

"Therefore, friends, when you are with us you too must obey him. To admit the need for weapons is to deny the might of Gova – and that is heresy."

Cyrus was floundering, divided between annoyance and incomprehension. The man's theatrical manner of speaking irritated him. So did his strange vocabulary – what on earth did "heresy" mean? "Then, Ozlam, you give us no choice but to leave," he sighed.

The High Father shook his head. "Not yet, friends. You have yet to taste our hospitality. The gates are closed against you, Cyrus, my child. Welcome to the Children of Go –"

Taja had heard enough. Who was this self-important show-off to tell them what they could and could not do? The situation called for a display of force, even if the target was a fellow Constant.

"Open the gates, Ozlam!" she demanded, fitting an arrow to her bow and aiming it at the High Father's chest. The watching crowd let out a gasp of horrified disbelief. "Go on, order them to be opened again – or you will be a dead man!"

"I – will – be – a – dead – man," echoed Ozlam slowly. "And to judge by the number of winters Gova seems to have blessed you with, lady, you yourself will soon be dead. Ah! What is death, eh? Death has no terrors for me, lady. I do the will of Gova." He spread wide his arms. "Kill me! Kill us all!"

Cyrus placed a hand on Taja's arm. "No need for that, Taja. You and the others keep them off while I open the gates again."

As Cyrus turned put his plan into action, Ozlam raised his hands and called out to the two men who had operated the gate handles, "Dismiss!"

Immediately a pair of odd-looking objects, each like a blackened tube, flew high over the fence and landed on top of the pile of bones on the other side.

Ignoring this action, Cyrus reached out to grasp the bare metal handles. "No!" screamed Roxanne. "Don't touch them! Get back, Cyrus!"

She alone of the Constants understood what was lying on the bones beyond the wire, so near and yet so distant. It was insulation. After closing the gates, the keepers had slipped the thick plastic sleeves off the handles and kept hold of them. At Ozlam's command, they had now thrown them over the fence. That left the unprotected steel handles as live as the rest of the fence: anyone touching them would die instantly.

Startled by Roxanne's urgency, Cyrus took a step backwards. Ozlam looked slightly surprised, disappointed even, as if he had hoped to see the visitor die as a warning to the others. "You understand the power of Gova?" he asked slowly, turning to Roxanne.

She frowned. "Yes and no, Ozlam." She wondered how much she should admit to knowing. A fatal current of electricity ran through the fence, she realised, but she had no idea how the Children of Gova put it there or why they spoke of "Gova" as if it were some sort of magic. Instinct told her to be careful. For all their talk about peace, Ozlam and his henchmen – like all fanatics – were plainly merciless.

"Yes – and – no," repeated the High Father. He studied Roxanne closely, unsure what to make of her. "You are very clever, lady…"

"Roxanne. My name's Roxanne, from the Constants of Yonne."

"Thank you, though I know not such people. Well, Roxanne, you and I need to talk together. Later. For the moment, would you please explain to our other guests that there is now no way out of our settlement? Once that is understood, you will surrender your instruments of cruelty and violence to Gova so we may grant you our customary hospitality."

In her mind, Roxanne ran through the sequence of events they had just witnessed. The gates shutting – the gatekeepers removing the insulation – the command "Dismiss!" – the instant obedience. Had the operation been rehearsed or even performed on a previous occasion? If it had, then how had the insulation got back…

Whatever was going on, Roxanne decided, brute strength was not the answer. "I will speak to my companions, High Father," she replied graciously. "They must understand the power of, er, Gova."

"Thank you, wise child Roxanne," chanted Ozlam with eyes that flickered more with uncertainty than gratitude.

While Roxanne and Ozlam had been trying to figure each other out, Cyrus, Taja and Navid were holding a whispered council of war. Not surprisingly, it got them nowhere. The fence had some deadly force they didn't understand. How had the operators managed to open the gates? What had they thrown over the wall? And why had Roxanne warned Cyrus against touching the handles? None of it made sense. At this stage, although all three Tallins were unimpressed with the behaviour of the Children of Gova, they had to accept that their weird hosts had their guests completely where they wanted them.

Roxanne hurried over to the Tallins. "Listen. I don't know much more than you do, but stay away from that fence. It'll kill you if you touch the metal. If you don't believe me, just take another look at those bones on the other side."

Navid nodded. "Yeah. Seems to have done for them alright. So how do we get out of here, Roxanne?"

"We don't. At least, not for the moment. All we can do is go along with this Ozlam and hope there's…"

"You mean hand over our weapons?" interrupted Navid.

Roxanne gave a resigned smile. "I'm afraid there's no alternative, Navid. Even if we killed all of them – and I don't think any of us want that – we'd still be stuck inside here."

"Then the Soterion Mission would be at an end," added Cyrus, "and we would've failed. If we do play along with them, Roxy, you reckon there's a way out?"

She tried to hide her uncertainty. "I don't know, Cy. We can only hope."

"Huh!" snorted Taja. "You bring us here because you hope there's a Soterion. You hope you won't die before we reach it. You hope Timur and his Zeds won't catch us up. And now you hope we can get out of this place! Come on, smooth-talking

Roxanne! It's time you swapped all that hoping for a bit of knowing, isn't it?"

"Shut up, Taja!" snapped Cyrus, genuinely angry. "That doesn't get us anywhere!"

"Nor does anything else, Cyrus," chipped in Navid. "At least these Gova guys seem to have got something that keeps them safe. If you ask me, I wouldn't mind one of those magic fences back in Della Tallis."

It was like the scene over the body of the dying Zavar, except worse. The rift between Taja and Roxanne had reopened, and Navid seemed to be having second thoughts about the whole enterprise. Divided and depressed, the small band of Constants had no choice but to do as the Children of Gova asked.

They surrendered their weapons to a posse of three eager boys, none of whom could have seen more than eleven winters. Their leader, a spritely fellow with the expression of a startled field mouse, grinned broadly at the new arrivals, nodded and ran off with his loot. The tools of war, Ozlam explained, would be destroyed on a fire. He then announced that dogs, animals associated only with Zeds, were not permitted to roam free within the settlement.

Corby was led off to be housed in a special hut. He would be well looked after, one of the twelve bearded men assured Navid, and returned to them when they left. Navid demanded to know when that would be. The man muttered weakly that it was up to the High Father, and Navid was too miserable to argue. Instead, he thought about Zavar and how such a noble friend appeared to have given up his life for nothing.

As the visitors were being led down the road towards the buildings at the centre of the settlement, the crowd at the gate fell in behind them. At first, the only sound was the shuffling of feet along the dusty track. Then a lone voice rang out, "As the Prophets taught us, let us sing!"

Immediately, they all began to chant. "Glory to Gova! Polish the Panel!" they sang, over and over again. "Glory to Gova! Polish the Panel! Glory to Gova! Polish the Panel!"

Cyrus looked at Roxanne in astonishment. "Eh? What the Della's this?" he asked. "Ever heard anything like it before, Roxy? What's going on?"

"I'm trying to work it out, Cy," she replied slowly. "It's puzzling. The singing reminds me of something from the Third Book of Yonne. If I remember rightly, there's a line of words in that book that reads, 'The chanting in the temple of Horus continued all night long.' I think that's what these people are doing: chanting, like the Long Dead used to do in buildings they called 'temples'."

Cyrus frowned. "What's this chanting for, Roxy? Is it supposed to scare away the Zeds?"

"Possibly. But it's more mysterious than that. We won't know for sure until we get to the Soterion."

"You really think we'll make it?"

She took his hand in hers. "Still believe in me, Cy?"

"Of course!"

"Then we'll make it. I promise!" Cyrus hoped she was speaking from her head as well as from her heart.

If Roxanne had known more of the forces ranged against them, she may well have sounded less confident. Even if she and her companions did manage to break out of the smothering embrace of the Children of Gova, they would hardly be out of danger. Timur and his ruthless Zeds were rapidly closing in from behind, while ahead Jumshid and Sheza had already reached the River No-Man in order to destroy the bridge.

Roxanne had one great advantage over her captors. Unlike them, she knew the true nature of the mystical force that kept them safe and which they treated with such exaggerated respect. Using information from the Books of Yonne and what she had learned of the Great Death, she was gradually piecing together an explanation of the Children of Gova and their extraordinary ways.

Obviously, she reasoned, like other Constant settlements, this one must have been set up during the last days of the Long Dead. Presumably a group of them, desperate to save the next generation from the lawlessness rapidly overtaking the world, had found this fertile patch of ground with its natural spring, and surrounded it with a high metal fence. They had then electrified it with a current strong enough to kill any living thing that touched it. That explained the piles of dead Zeds around the perimeter.

At this point, Roxanne's thesis became a bit sketchy. Nearly all the items in the *IKEA Catalogue* were powered either from something the Long Dead called "batteries" or from a "plug". Neither of these had she seen in the settlement. There was another possibility, however.

A few devices in the *Catalogue* were said to operate on "solar power". Yonne scholars had worked out that this meant the power of the sun. Roxanne thought back to the huge mirror-like object they had noticed when they first looked down on the settlement. Could that be a way of capturing the power of the sun and turning it into electricity? If so, it would explain the "Polish the Panel" chant – probably half-remembered instructions given by the Long Dead.

Although she was able to figure out a plausible explanation for the technology of the place, Roxanne found it much harder to understand its behaviour. What was all this "Gova" business? And why "holy" and "heresy"? The latter two words she understood from the Third Book of Yonne. They were associated with religion, a subject that had divided the settlement's best minds for generations. The concept was not in the *Catalogue* or in *Peter Pan*, but it cropped up a lot in the Third Book. The best Roxanne could make of it was that it was the Long Dead's way of explaining what was beyond reason.

She turned the idea over in her mind for a few moments. Then, grabbing hold of Cyrus' arm, she exclaimed, "That's it, Cy!"

Cyrus had never seen her so animated. "That's what, Roxy?"

She lowered her voice. "I think I get what's going on here."

"Go on, then, enlighten us with your great wisdom," teased Cyrus, cheered by her sudden enthusiasm. "And let's hope it helps us get out of here. Soon."

"It might." Roxanne looked around cautiously. "It also might make our position even more difficult. I don't reckon truth is something these people are too keen on."

"So? What is it?"

"As I said, Cy, it's pretty complicated and will take a lot of explaining. I'll leave it until we're all together, without any twitching ears listening in."

"That dubious, is it?"

"Dubious, yes. But it's also what our charming host would call 'heresy'."

"Meaning?"

"Meaning it'd probably give him an excuse to lock us up or even have us done away with."

By now, they had arrived at the heart of the village. Here, to their further annoyance, the men and women were taken to separate quarters. Escorts led Cyrus and Navid to a small hut to the left of the main hall where they were given water for washing and fed vegetables, fruit and nuts. As animals did not get past the fence, no Child of Gova had ever tasted meat. After they had eaten, the two Tallins were asked to step outside for a talk with one of the twelve men dressed in yellow who had stood next to Ozlam at the gate. He explained that toga-wearers, like himself, were "Magi", the self-appointed high officials of the Children of Gova. It was a pleasure, he continued, to welcome new members into a community whose numbers had been falling recently. Cyrus considered asking why he was so sure he and his friends would stay, but decided against it. It wouldn't get them anywhere. For the time being, Ozlam and his oddly-dressed cronies very much held the whip hand.

In a hut on the other side of the hall, Roxanne and Taja were treated in a similar manner except that, when it came to the talk, three Magi separated them and escorted Roxanne alone into the hall itself. On the way in, seeing a faded enamel notice on the wall, she stopped to read it. The move was noticed at once.

"What are you doing, Roxanne?" rolled a familiar voice from the far end of the room. Roxanne looked up. There, bolt upright in a large chair, sat Ozlam, High Father of the Children of Gova. Roxanne walked towards him, saying nothing.

"Tell me, child, what it was you were doing?"

"I was looking at the pictures, Ozlam," Roxanne replied carefully. "The wonderful pictures."

The interior of the hall was certainly a blaze of colour. Every surface except the floor was decorated with images of the sun. Whether these pictures were wonderful or not was a matter of taste. Scratched, splashed and scribbled, she thought most looked like the sort of work young children did back in Yonne.

Ozlam was not convinced by Roxanne's calm response. "You were not looking at the thing on the wall, near the door?"

"No. What is it?"

"It is a relic of the Prophets. It is known as writing. Those marks are words and people who can read understand what they mean." Ozlam leaned forward in his chair and stared hard at Roxanne. "Are you sure you cannot read, Roxanne?"

"No, I cannot read." Roxanne's face might have remained calm, but inside she was churning. Lies did not come easily to her. Worse, she did not like this man one bit and, as he was making clear, he obviously felt the same about her.

"You are lying to me, child. It is not wise to tell lies to the High Father. I was observing you when you first entered our community." Ozlam's slow, chanting tone suddenly quickened and grew louder. "You knew what the others did not. You knew about Gova! How? Tell me, child! How?"

"In Yonne, where I come from, I once heard a woman – one of those able to read – talk about something she called electricity – "

The word seemed to strike Ozlam like a physical blow. Leaping to his feet, he screamed, "Heresy! We have a heretic in our midst." The Magi who had been standing by the walls watching the interview, sprang forward and seized Roxanne by the arms. She did not resist.

"What have I done wrong, Ozlam?" she cried. "Tell me!"

The High Father came down from the platform on which his chair stood like a throne and placed himself directly in front of her. "Heretic!" he spat. "You dared to say that word!"

How could Roxanne have known what had taken place twenty-eight years earlier? The settlement had given shelter to two literate Constants fleeing from the Zeds. Once inside the gates and realising what was going on, the new arrivals had begun openly mocking the whole Gova idea, telling the crowd that their real guardian was electricity. The men were swiftly incarcerated and buried alive – the Children of Gova's supposedly non-violent method of execution. Nevertheless, the very foundations of the community had been shaken. Two generations passed before the heresy was stamped out and, ever since that time, no one except the High Fathers and the Gova's

Magi had even whispered the word "electricity".

If Roxanne was in serious trouble for her words, what happened next sealed her fate. Struggling against the men who held her and begging Ozlam to listen, she shook aside the lock of hair that hid her scarred forehead.

The High Father stared in disbelief. "Great Gova defend us!" he cried. "Not only a heretic – but a Zed! A damned, cursed Zed in our midst! Bury her! Bury her at dawn. As Gova rises, so shall she go down!"

Still begging for a fair hearing, the weeping Roxanne was dragged from the room. Shortly afterwards, Cyrus, Navid and Taja were seized and tied up. They were under arrest, the guards said, for secretly introducing a heretic Zed into the community.

That same evening, things were getting equally tense on the banks of the No-Man. On this stage, however, there were only two characters. Unable to see the bridge they had been told to destroy, Jumshid and Sheza stared up and down the river wondering what had happened.

"Bridge gone," repeated Jumshid several times. "Bridge gone."

It was Sheza, benefiting from the tuition he had received from Constant prisoners, who finally worked out what had gone wrong.

"No, Jum-Jum Dumb-Dumb!" he cried. "The bridge is not gone. We are on the riverbank, but in the wrong place."

Jumshid frowned. What did that irritating cub mean? "Wrong place?" he grumbled. "What you meaning 'wrong place', Sheza?"

"I mean, Dumb-Dumb," sneered Timur's appointed heir, delighting in the rhyme he had just invented, "I mean the bridge is where it was. We – Sheza and Jumshid – we are in the wrong place. Not the right part of the river." Jabbing a filthy finger at his temple, he added, "Got it, Dumb-Dumb?"

Jumshid bit his bottom lip. He was getting annoyed. Of course he had got it. The bridge was further upstream from where they were now. "Yeah, cub," he said, grinding his few remaining teeth. "Bridge along there." The captain raised his right arm and pointed firmly upstream.

Sheza thought for a few moments. He fixed his gaze on Jumshid's arm, then at the green, slow-flowing river. Eventually, he raised his left arm, pointed downstream and declared, "Jum-Jum Dumb-Dumb wrong. Again. The bridge is that way."

For a long time the two men stood in silence, pointing in opposite directions like strangely carved signposts. Sheza cracked first.

"You are wrong, Jumshid!" he shouted, slapping his left hand back against his side.

The older man remained unmoved. "How many winters Sheza see?" he asked. "Young cub not know. Jumshid knows. Been here before, so he is right."

"I will prove it! Come with me, this way," screamed Sheza. "I order you!" He set off at a brisk walk along the bank, following the current downstream.

Jumshid did not move. After about a hundred paces, Sheza stopped and listened. Nothing, no footsteps following him. Very slowly, fury rising within him, he turned. There was the captain, his outstretched arm still pointing obstinately upstream, in exactly the same position as he had left him.

"Traitor! Why don't you follow me?"

"'Cos you is wrong and Jumshid is right. Simple."

"I am not wrong, Dumb-Dumb!"

"Yes, you is. Baby Lamb!"

"What did you say?"

"Jumshid say Sheza is Baby Lamb. He never be Malik of Grozny like Timur! Baby Lamb! Baa-baa! Baa-baa!"

The taunting was too much for the spoilt, hot-headed Sheza. Screaming like a stuck pig, he charged along the bank and hurled himself into the captain's midriff. With a revolting hiss, the polluted contents of the man's lungs were forced into the atmosphere, and for a few moments the winded captain stood with his hands on his knees, gasping for air.

Sheza began to giggle. "Poor Jum-Jum Dumb-Dumb too old to figh –"

The sentence was never finished. Rising with the speed of a striking snake, Jumshid cracked both his fists into his opponent's face, breaking his nose and sending him reeling backwards into a patch of scrub.

The fight was on.

6
Disaster

With their hands tied behind their backs and roped together like slaves, Cyrus, Taja and Navid were led into Gova Hall by a troupe of wispy-faced Magi. Here, where a short while previously Ozlam had sentenced Roxanne to death, they were made to sit on the concrete floor. The High Father was on his way to speak to them, they were told.

When Ozlam appeared, he did so slowly, slipping onto the platform at the far end of the hall and standing, hands raised, for some time without speaking. Every move he makes, thought Cyrus, every word he utters is carefully planned to give the impression of wisdom and maturity: his slow, sing-song speech, his flamboyant hand gestures, even his robe and full beard – they were all part of a grand charade. High Father or not, Ozlam was before everything else an actor.

"Visitors, guests, friends," he began, lowering his arms and advancing with measured steps towards the three prisoners, "you have broken my heart!"

Cyrus resisted the temptation to say something rude. Beside him, though, he noticed that Navid was gazing at the speaker with a strange intensity. Taja, sitting on his other side, remained her usual inscrutable self.

"I repeat," chanted Ozlam, walking right up to the trio until he hung over them like a malevolent tree, "you have broken my poor heart! It has been riven in two pieces, like a tree cloven by lightning, by the cruel deception of those whom we took in from the wilderness. We gave them food, we gave them shelter, we gave them kindness – and how did they respond? By bringing with them, like a clawed scorpion hidden beneath their clothing, a vile and most foul Zed!"

Cyrus could take no more. "That's not true, Ozlam!" he shouted. "And you know it! Roxanne isn't a Zed. Look at her scar! Does it look as if it's been there since childhood? Anyway, where is she? What have you done with her?"

Ozlam's eyes narrowed slightly. "The heretic is with us, Cyrus. And I have, of course, observed her scar: the mark of the Zed is indeed a new one. But who put it there, Cyrus? Tell me that."

"It was the work of Timur, Malik of the Grozny. She was his prisoner before she escaped and came to us." Even as he was speaking, Cyrus was aware how unconvincing he sounded. The evidence he needed – the steady, honest gaze of Roxanne's green eyes – was not to hand.

"I see," responded Ozlam. "You were there, too, were you? You were also a prisoner of these Grozny and saw what actually happened?"

Cyrus shook his head. "Ah!" sighed Ozlam, clasping his hands together and smiling. "So this woman with a Zed tattoo came to you with a sad story – and you believed her? Well, why did you, Cyrus?"

"Because of her manner, because I just know she is honest," said Cyrus desperately.

Ozlam shook his head and turned to Navid. "I hear your name is Navid?"

"Yes, er, High Father."

Cyrus looked at him sharply. What was all this "High Father" business? Couldn't Navid see the man was a poser and a bully?

"The name 'Navid' is pleasing," chanted Ozlam with an empty smile. "So, friend Navid, you too believed Roxanne's story?"

"Yeah. Well, yeah. Like Cyrus said, she seemed a good sort of person, someone we could trust, and he usually gets these things right, High Father." Cyrus winced inwardly at the repetition of the title but said nothing.

"Seemed good…Mmm, yes. She does seem good, doesn't she, Navid? Nevertheless, we Children of Gova prefer matters to be clearer. As clear as the might of the Great Gova himself."

"Eh?" frowned Navid.

"Surely you remember our fence?"

"Of course. It's amazing."

"Amazing, certainly. A strong and visible sign of the mighty and mysterious strength of the Great Gova who keeps us safe day after day, moon after moon, winter after winter, generation after generation. And all we have to do is polish the mirror and

111

give him thanks. Think about that, Navid. Think about that."

Navid did not reply, but when Cyrus looked at him again, he saw the same far-away expression on his friend's face, almost as if he were in a trance.

To Cyrus' surprise and alarm, Taja was more outspoken. Yes, she told Ozlam, she had had doubts about Roxanne from the beginning. One always had to be careful of strangers in case they were spies or traitors.

"Be quiet, Taja!" Cyrus burst out. "Think of Roxanne!"

"That is precisely what she is doing," cut in Ozlam. "It looks to me as if you have allowed this Z-marked woman to cast a spell on you."

Cyrus struggled in vain to loosen the rope that held his wrists. "Rubbish! It's you who are casting a spell, Ozlam! You won't accept what she says because of what she knows. She understands what we don't."

"She is a heretic!"

"What does that mean? She warned me not to touch the fence, remember? Yes, she knows something about it." Then, struggling to figure out what Roxanne knew and infuriated by his interrogator's stubbornness, Cyrus blurted out, "She's cleverer than you! She can see through this Gova rubbish, and she can read – "

"Ah!" interrupted Ozlam. "Thank you. Another lie! She told me she was not able to read."

Cyrus lowered his head. Oh, no! What had he done? He had betrayed the one person…How could he have been so foolish? Oh, Roxy! I'm so sorry. Forgive me, please.

"You won't hurt her, will you?" Cyrus said quietly, deciding further argument was futile.

The irony of the remark was not lost on Ozlam and his mouth twisted into a half-smile. Although his prisoners knew Roxanne was being held, they did not know sentence had already been passed on her.

"You forget, Cyrus, the Children of Gova are a peaceful people," he said calmly. "Just as we do not possess weapons, so we do no violence. No, your Roxanne will not be hurt."

"Thank you. And she will be returned to us soon?"

The High Father made no direct reply. Saying only "All will be revealed", he turned and walked from the hall.

The three prisoners said not a word as they were led away to a small hut on the edge of the village. Night was falling fast and from somewhere near the hall a single male voice started to chant. It was an eerie, moaning sound, not regular like the singing of the crowd on the way back from the gate, but rising and falling like the wind. On and on it went, till the last glow of daylight had drained from the sky and a sheen of cold moonlight lit the bleak concrete shapes of the settlement.

Within their place of detention, the captive Constants lay on their beds of dried grass and tried in vain to sleep. Above the locked door, the iron bars in the only window threw sinister silhouettes across the floor. Outside, the mournful chant continued without a break. Cyrus, who had been trying desperately to contain his frustration and annoyance, finally burst out, "Taja, why did you say that to Ozlam?"

"I wondered when you would ask, Cyrus. Isn't it obvious?"

He sat up, casting a long dark shadow across the room. "No, it's not! Here we are, locked up by these crazy Gova people who've taken Roxanne goodness knows where – and then you say she might be a Zed! We've been over all that, haven't we? It was hardly the time to stick a knife in her back. Remember why we're here, Taja: the whole mission's pointless without her."

"Cyrus, Cyrus, Cyrus!" purred Taja. "Relax! Do you think that shouting at Ozlam, like you did, was going to do any good? It only annoyed him."

"I was telling the truth, Taja. And I was doing it for Roxanne."

"And look what happened. By revealing that she was literate, you got her still deeper into trouble. Even Navid was more subtle than that."

"Was I? I don't remember. Like Cyrus, I just spoke up straight."

"Oh, come on, Nav!" snapped Cyrus, feeling increasingly isolated and miserable. "You told Ozlam this place was amazing."

"Well, the fence is amazing, Cy, isn't it? Brilliant." He paused for a moment, listening to the chant reverberating through the still night air. "You know, I actually could live here. Might actually get used to this funny singing they do. Quite relaxing."

"Nav, don't be so stupid!" Cyrus was genuinely worried. "Anyway, you couldn't stay here because of Corby. No animals, remember?"

Navid yawned. "Oh, yeah! Well, what I mean is, I could live here if Corby wasn't around. And Roxanne, of course."

"Well, they are," replied Cyrus. "So that's it, OK?"

"I suppose so. 'Night, Cy! 'Night, Taja! Hope Roxanne's alright." With that, Navid turned on his side and was soon asleep.

A while later, when Taja moved over and laid a hand on Cyrus' shoulder, he shrugged it off.

"Relax, Cyrus," she said quietly. "It's not that bad."

Isn't it? he thought. He lay back and gazed up at the moonlight flooding in through the window. It couldn't be much worse. Far from home, held captive by lunatics, Zavar dead, Taja being impossible, Navid coming up with those ridiculous ideas about staying here – and, worst of all, Roxanne stolen from him. He had known her only a matter of days and yet he missed her badly.

"Please be alright, Roxy," he mouthed silently to himself, "and come back safe. Please!" Although he knew nothing of the concept, it was almost as if he were praying.

On the banks of the slow-flowing River No-Man, Sheza was also in need of comfort. He was regretting having ever picked a fight with so tough an opponent as Captain Jumshid. He might have been lighter and quicker, but these qualities were more than matched by the older man's strength and experience.

Having picked himself out of the thorny scrub into which the Captain's first blow had deposited him, Sheza found that skipping round Jumshid and taunting him with "Jum-Jum Dumb-Dumb" was both exhausting and ineffective. At some point, he had to close with his enemy and inflict serious damage.

Jumshid was also aware that it was up to Sheza to make a

move, and he decided it would be on his terms. Somewhere to their right, a bird cried. The Captain deliberately flicked his eyes in the direction of the noise. It was a simple yet effective trick. Seeing what he thought was an opening, Sheza darted forward and aimed a vicious kick at Jumshid's groin.

The Captain was waiting. With surprising agility for a large man, he grabbed the young man's ankle in both hands, and gave a sharp twist to the left. A tendon-snapping crack was followed by a screech of pain. With a desperate heave, Sheza snatched his leg away and stepped backwards. The damaged knee instantly collapsed and he rolled headlong into the scrub for a second time.

"Who dumb-dumb now, Baby Lamb?" panted the Captain. "Jumshid winner, eh?"

Sheza lay there, breathing heavily and wiping away the blood streaming from his crumpled nose. The pain in his leg was excruciating. There was no way he'd be able to defeat this man in a straight fight, especially now he had taken such a battering. Deceit was the answer. What was it Timur had once said to him? "Clever lies take the prize." That was it. He could still win, but he had to do it by cunning.

"Yes, Captain Jumshid," he said, rising painfully to his feet, "you win. I will go your way, up the river."

The Captain eyed him suspiciously. He might not have had Sheza's education sessions, but he had been appointed to command because he was capable of thinking for himself. More or less. And like all Zeds who survived into their nineteenth year, he had learned to trust no one and be ready for anything at any time of night or day.

Animal instinct told him that Sheza was bent on swift revenge for his humiliation. Staring hard into his young rival's blood-spattered face, the Captain made a plan.

"Good," he muttered. "Baby Lamb see sense, eh?" Sheza nodded sullenly. "I show the way," Jumshid added. "You come following."

Picking up his weapon, a huge club with an iron spike embedded in the end, the Captain lumbered off along the bank, going upstream. Sheza grabbed his bow and limped painfully off in pursuit.

Jumshid reckoned it would take Sheza about twenty paces to draw an arrow from the quiver on his back, fit it to his bow, pull back the string, steady himself, take careful aim and…

Pretending to trip on a root, the Captain flung himself to the ground. His timing was perfect. The arrow sped over where his body had been moments earlier and splashed harmlessly into the river behind.

The veteran warrior sprang to his feet and turned to confront his would-be assassin. Sheza, trembling violently, struggled to pull another arrow from his quiver. "Er, shooting bird – for food," he stammered. The second arrow fell impotently to the ground from his shaking fingers.

"Food?" bellowed Jumshid, tearing down the bank like an angry bear. "You be the food, Baby Lamb! Food for crockendiles!"

Swiping away the knife that Sheza had drawn to protect himself, the Captain grasped his opponent round the waist and squeezed. Ribs cracked like dry chicken bones. When the

117

breath had been almost entirely crushed from the body, Jumshid dropped it to the ground like a sack of logs and stood over it, grinning.

Sheza was now too weak, too broken, to resist. Ignoring his pitiful moans, the Captain stretched out huge fists, grasped his human trophy by the hair and belt, and raised it high above his head. He held the pose for a few triumphant seconds. Finally, with a roar of victory and a mighty heave, he tossed the body far into the grey-brown stream.

The end came very quickly. Sheza resurfaced and splashed feebly towards the shore for a few strokes before the fan of sinister ripples closed in on him. There followed a short scream, a moment of furious thrashing, then silence. The only sign that Sheza had ever been on this planet was a small red stain upon the tranquil waters. By the time Jumshid had picked up his club and resumed his journey, even that had disappeared.

Cyrus was woken by the sound of the bar on the other side of the door being drawn back. The chanting, he noticed, had stopped. The door opened and one of the Magi entered, his cloaked silhouette sharp against the orange-blue of the dawn.

"Tell me where she is," he demanded briskly. "And the dog."

It took a few seconds for the questions to register. Navid was first to react. "What do you mean, 'dog'?" he muttered, sitting up and feeling in vain for the axe that he had always kept at his bedside.

"The heretic and the dog have disappeared."

Another Magus appeared in the doorway. "The High Father

says it is your doing. You must tell us where they are."

By now Taja and Cyrus were wide awake and on their feet. "Wait a moment," said Cyrus, wiping the sleep from his eyes and running his fingers through his tousled brown hair. "You yourselves removed Roxanne and Corby, Navid's dog, and now you ask us where they are…Is this some kind of joke?"

The Magus who had been first to enter made a scornful sound through his teeth. "The Children of Gova do not joke. We are serious people and –"

"I want my dog!" shouted Navid, rushing over to the man and grabbing the front of his robe. "Where's Corby? Tell me!"

Cyrus and Taja pulled him back before he could harm the startled man, and the second Magus resumed the explanation. "The heretic, the Zed woman you know as Roxanne –"

"She's not a Zed!" interrupted Cyrus. "How many times do I have to tell you?"

The Magus gave him a look that was part apprehension, part contempt. "You do not know, but the High Father had decreed that the heretic should die this morning –"

Cyrus opened his mouth in disbelief. "What did you say?" he growled, striding up to the man and almost spitting the words in his face. "Repeat those words, you freak – if you dare!"

The two Magi stepped back and glanced nervously at each other. "Violence is not the way of Gova," stammered the first.

"Hang your Gova! Hang him on that evil fence of yours!" yelled Cyrus, finally giving voice to the thoughts that had been building from the moment the gate had slammed behind them. "You're mad, all of you! Do you hear? You're twisted! More like

Zeds than true Constants!"

"Take heed lest you too fall into the pit of heresy, Cyrus," said a familiar voice from outside the door. It was Ozlam. "Control your fury and hear the High Father of the Children of Gova," he continued, coming into the room and standing next to the Magi. "I will enlighten you."

Taja, who until this moment had kept quiet, urged Cyrus and Navid, for all their sakes, to hold back until they had heard what Ozlam had to say. He thanked her and resumed his explanation.

The previous evening, when glorious Gova had retired to sleep, Roxanne had been taken to the prison chamber to await her sentence. Yes, as the Magus had said, she would have been executed in the morning.

Cyrus swore. "Sanctimonious liar!" he went on. "And you said no violence. Huh! I promise you, if she hasn't got out and you really have killed her, it'll be your turn next. As painfully as I can manage, too!"

Ozlam remained curiously unruffled. Resuming, he said that, contrary to Cyrus' accusation, he had not lied when he said no violence would be used against Roxanne: burying alive – "interment" he called it – would simply have involved shovelling earth on to her. That was hardly a violent act, was it?

"So what happened?" asked Cyrus, still shaking with rage.

This morning, Ozlam said, before the rising of Gova, a pair of Magi had gone to the chamber in which Roxanne was being held. She was not there. The door remained locked, but she had vanished. Shortly afterwards, they found Corby was also missing. If the other members of the mission had not freed the heretic, she must have managed somehow to get away on her own and was now making her way back to rejoin the Zeds. She was taking them a present, too: a fine hunting dog named Corby.

A stunned silence followed Ozlam's speech. All three Tallins struggled to make sense of it. Cyrus felt it most deeply. He was pretty sure Ozlam was lying and that Roxanne and Corby had both been secretly done away with. But what if the story were true? If Roxanne had managed to get out of the prison, wouldn't she also have tried to release them? The fact that she hadn't might mean Taja's suspicions had been right all along: Roxanne really was a Zed spy, a traitor who had deliberately entrapped him. It was too painful to contemplate.

In the end, Cyrus realised, it didn't matter which version of events he believed. Whether she was dead or had run away, Roxanne had gone. That intense, fleeting joy, the most powerful emotion he had ever felt, was over. The smile that had stirred his heart, the kindly light behind those glorious green eyes, the laughter as she had tried to teach him to read, the hand in the darkness...None of it ever again. No more Roxy.

As if battered by physical blows, Cyrus covered his face with his hands and crumpled to his knees. What had he done? He had abandoned his community and most of his friends, thrown away a promising career, broken the principles he had sworn to uphold – for an insubstantial dream. For nothing.

What happened during the rest of the day, he neither noticed nor cared. Ozlam and the Magi went out and the door was rebarred. Later, he was aware of Navid coming over and speaking to him. Shortly afterwards, the door opened and

Navid left. All this time, Taja said nothing. He was conscious only of her sitting quietly beside him.

By mid-afternoon, Cyrus was beginning to focus his thoughts again. He was hungry and wolfed down the plate of bread and fruit brought by the Magi. After that, as his head gradually cleared, he talked to Taja. He started by asking where Navid was. Had they taken him off to be buried alive next to Roxanne?

The truth was, if anything, worse. Devastated by the loss of Corby and the failure of the mission, Navid had decided to become a Child of Gova. At first, Cyrus couldn't believe it. Then he remembered his friend's trance-like expression when listening to Ozlam and what he had said about living in this settlement if there were no Roxanne or Corby…

Cyrus' thoughts turned to Salama, Navid's wedun back in Della Tallis. She might have had their second child by now. How would she feel if she knew what had happened? The only consolation was that, when she agreed to Navid going on the mission, she must have known there was a good chance he would never come back. Even so, Cyrus hoped she never learned the true reason for her man's disappearance.

The more they talked, the more Cyrus' hatred of Ozlam and his Children of Gova grew. The Zeds were wicked, yes, but in a different, direct way. Their cruelty, though despicable, was straightforward. In this place, evil was hidden beneath a cloak of goodness, which somehow made it worse. Navid, the true and honest friend he had known all his life, the man who had previously put his duty to the Constant cause before everything else, had been lured away by ridiculous talk of magic and Gova

122

and polishing the panel. It was shameful, truly shameful.

Cyrus' thoughts went back to Roxanne. She had known the truth about this place, hadn't she? Perhaps that was why she… No, it was impossible.

"Taja," he asked eventually, looking up at his one remaining companion, "what do you think really happened to – well, you know who?"

"Roxanne?"

"Yes, Roxanne."

"I'm sorry to say it, Cyrus, but I was probably right all along." She spoke so reluctantly, with so much understanding, that for the first time Cyrus wondered whether he should have paid more attention to her from the beginning. Her judgement had generally been sound on previous occasions.

"You don't honestly think they've buried her, do you?" Taja continued.

"That Ozlam's capable of anything."

"Maybe. But don't you think those Magi who came here this morning sounded genuine?"

"Perhaps. Yet what if Ozlam had lied to them?" Cyrus saw where her line of reasoning was leading and was trying not to follow.

Taja shook her head. "That little group, Ozlam and his Magi, seem to run the place. The only other people we've seen helping out were those boys who ran off with our weapons. They're probably future Magi under training." She sighed. "No. The only real possibility is that your friend found out what she wanted – about us or about this place – and is now passing it on to Timur."

The mention of Timur reminded Cyrus of what Roxanne had said in her sleep on the day she arrived in Della Tallis. He couldn't imagine for one second that she had anything but detestation for the leader of the Grozny Zeds. On the other hand, might he have some sort of unspoken hold over her? Could she have agreed to act as his spy to avoid further torture? Even the bravest human beings have their breaking points...Poor Roxy! It was just possible, he supposed. Anything was now possible.

"You remember how she told you not to touch the gates, Cyrus?"

"Of course."

"Well, that was after those bits of plastic had been thrown over the fence, wasn't it?"

"I've thought of that," said Cyrus. "She understood the power of the fence, didn't she? There's something she didn't have time to tell us."

"Which means she may have worked out how to escape."

Cyrus shook his head, still refusing to accept Taja's cruel logic. "She was locked in a room. How did she get out of that?"

Taja shrugged. "No idea, Cyrus. But we don't have to worry, do we? It's just you and me now. Like it was before." A smile flickered across her face. "Just you and me."

Cyrus looked into her black eyes. There was one matter he had to get straight. "Taja, tell me honestly why you joined this mission."

She tossed her curls of ebony hair and laughed. "I've told you, Cyrus. I didn't trust Roxanne and..." She paused, expressionless, staring him straight in the face.

"Go on."

"You know the answer. I came to be with you."

"Oh, Taja!" he sighed, shaking his head. "You shouldn't have done it, should you?"

"Why not? I'm not made of wood, Cyrus. Yes, there are some things I can't control. Besides, it was worth it. I've got you all to myself now, haven't I?"

Cyrus turned away and said nothing. Her tone alarmed him more than her words. It had sounded so confident, so sure of itself, almost obsessed. Shocked, he realised it reminded him of another voice he had heard a lot of recently.

Never had Cyrus felt this low. Everything he had set his heart on had crumbled away. He was in agonies of loss and uncertainty over the disappearance of Roxanne, wary of being by himself with Taja, and depressed by Navid's desertion and the failure of the Soterion Mission. Had he been left in this state, imprisoned and deeply sad, the suffocating blanket of his depression may have enfolded him entirely.

As it turned out, he was not alone with his melancholy for long. In the middle of the night, the door of the room where he and Taja were held opened silently to admit a most unexpected visitor.

Jumshid's geographical knowledge proved more accurate than Sheza's. After he had fed his rival to the crocodiles, he advanced quickly up the bank of the No-Man until, rounding a bend, he found himself staring at the broken ruins of the bridge with its central span of two rusting rails.

The Captain scratched his head. What were his orders? Break the bridge down or shoot anyone trying to cross. That should be easy enough, even though there was now just one of him. First, he'd have a go at destruction. If that didn't work, he'd position himself on the other side of the river and shoot dead anyone who set foot on the bridge. He grinned, congratulating himself on having picked up Sheza's bow. Timur would never know what had happened to its owner – and all the glory would be Jumshid's!

Choosing a comfortable tree to sleep in, the Captain settled down for the night. He would start work on the bridge in the morning.

While Jumshid was preparing to destroy the mission's escape route, Timur was supervising the other element of his plan. He was cheered by the discovery of Zavar's body, already rendered unrecognizable by the scavenging of birds and wild animals, because it told him he was now tracking four Constants, not five. That would make things easier when it came to a fight.

The settlement of the Children of Gova, which Timur came across shortly after they had found the remains of Zavar, presented a fresh problem. His dogs had picked up human scent near the edge of the canyon. He pondered the significance of this. Might it be Roxanne and her Tallin companions? Possibly. Well, if they had gone inside that murderous fence his quest was over and he could turn his mind to other matters. No one who passed through those shining gates ever came out again. On the other hand, the chances of his Constants having found the remote colony were slight. Even if they had, they were almost certainly too sensible to enter.

No, he concluded, whether the scent was that of the group he was after or not, it must be still ahead of him. Nevertheless, as a precaution he ordered two men to stay behind and report back to him immediately if they saw anything unusual. It wasn't a sensible plan. Having hung around the perimeter of the ravine for several days and seen nothing untoward, the men eventually wandered off with the intention of re-joining their tribe. Hopelessly lost, they died of thirst two weeks later.

Pressing on past the Gova settlement, Timur had spread the rest of his men out like a net, sweeping across the landscape. If the Constants got wind of where he was and tried to double back or flee to the side, his warriors would intercept them. With every moment that passed, the closer they came to the river and the tighter they drew the net. This time, he told himself, there would be no escape.

Nevertheless, getting Zeds to do anything other than fight was no easy matter, and keeping them in some sort of straight line was taxing Timur's leadership skills to the limit. Whipping those who strayed slowed the operation down too much. He had greater success rewarding those who stayed in line with a night among the breeding slaves. The idea worked as an incentive but an orgy of violation left the men slow and listless the following morning.

Nor was Timur helped by the absence of Sheza and Jumshid.

Both of them, although far from bright, would have been capable of taking control of part of the line. Still, the situation gave others an opportunity to show their mettle, and no one benefited from this more than Giv, the willing youth who had first come to the Malik's notice beside the stream.

Words are not exactly Giv's strength, Timur reflected one hot afternoon as they combed through an area of scattered thorn bushes, but he's loyal and keen. Somewhere, deep inside his thick skull, he probably has a brain, too. Quite a sharp one. Why, if Sheza fails me, I might do worse than train up Giv as my successor. In fact, I might prepare them both. Nothing like a bit of rivalry to keep a Zed on his toes.

Timur's musings were interrupted by shouting from the hill to his left. Though he needed to go and see what was going on personally, rapidity was tricky. To keep the sun off his pearly white skin when in the open, he was accompanied by four men holding a canopy of scarlet cloth above his head. Now, as he hurried up the slope in the direction of the noise, the bearers struggled to keep up with him.

"Quicker, snails!" he screeched as the men lurched this way and that across the rough ground. "And keep the shade over me, vermin, unless you want to cook your Malik!"

The ungainly procession had not gone far before Timur saw someone running down towards them. "Stop!" he cried. "Wait!"

As the figure drew closer, Timur recognised it as Giv.

"Malik!" the youth panted as he reached the canopy. "Giv seen! Giv seen!"

Timur rolled his eyes and heaved an exaggerated sigh.

Really, he must teach this mudbrain to speak. "Well, Giv, what have you seen?"

7
Old Friends, New Dangers

Taja woke first. She lay still for a few seconds until the dreary chanting reminded her where she was. At the same time, she became aware that someone or something was moving to her left. When she opened her eyes to see what it was, a grubby hand closed over her mouth.

"Shh! Don't say nothing, lady!"

She obeyed the command more out of surprise than fear. No one had ever spoken to her like this before – the term "lady" was almost unheard of in Della Tallis – and the hand that now withdrew respectfully from her face was small, much smaller than an adult's.

Cyrus, exhausted by the turmoil of the previous day, remained sound asleep. The stranger bent down and gently shook his shoulder. "Wake up, mister! Wake up!" Cyrus opened his eyes. What was going on? He blinked, glanced across at Taja, then peered up at the figure bending over him.

Although clouds filtered the full brilliance of the moon, there was sufficient light for Cyrus to make out a small, lean figure with a ball of black curly hair. He recognised him at once. It was the boy with the impish expression who, at Ozlam's command, had taken away their weapons to be burned.

The boy raised a finger to his lips and, with his other hand, beckoned Cyrus and Taja closer. "Want to get out?" he whispered.

Cyrus nodded, instinctively trusting the lad's eager tone. Taja was more cautious, "Who are you?" she hissed. "Is this some trick, because if it is – "

The boy shook his head vigorously. "We got no time," he said, his face suddenly furrowed with anxiety. "If we gets out, I'll explain. Promise. But we got to move quick." He made as if to stand.

Taja stopped him. "We? Are you coming with us?"

"Of course! You can't get out without me – and I can't get nowhere outside without you. See? You in or not?"

Taja looked across at Cyrus. "Well?"

"Please!" the boy urged in a tone that had changed suddenly from confident to pleading.

"Alright," said Cyrus. "Come on, Taja. Anything's better than staying here, isn't it?" He turned to the boy. "And what about our friend?"

"Which one?"

"Navid, the man who was with us when we came in. The one with the long shaggy hair."

"Oh, him! You think he wants to come too?" Cyrus nodded. "OK. I'll see what I can do. Follow me. We's mice, OK?"

Cyrus looked at Taja and smiled. The situation, although perilous, was also most bizarre.

As they passed through the door and advanced cautiously along the side of the building, Cyrus struggled to make sense of what was happening. Why was there no one around? Where were the guards? How could this eccentric boy get them through that deadly fence? For one accustomed to taking charge, he felt unsettlingly powerless, carried along by a current of strange events over which he had no control.

At the edge of the hut in which they had been held, the boy paused. Indicating to them to stay where they were, he sprinted across a dusty courtyard to what looked like a veranda. Taja and Cyrus watched as he inched along in front of it for a few paces before disappearing. In the gloom, Taja felt for Cyrus' hand and gave it a squeeze. He responded half-heartedly, wishing she would keep her hands to herself. The situation was complicated enough as it was.

Moments later, the boy came padding back across the courtyard. He shook his head. "Can't get to your friend," he whispered. "Guarded."

Cyrus' spirits sank once more. They had been lifted slightly by the thought of meeting up with Navid, though he might not be able to persuade him to join them – but now even that was impossible. He sighed and followed the others to the end of the building, across what seemed to be a street, and into the shadows of a windowless barn. The sound of the chanting was getting louder. The mystery deepened when the boy whispered "Gova" and signalled to them to look round the wall they were leaning against.

Taja went first, then Cyrus. There, some fifty paces away, was what looked like an enormous piece of shiny glass. In front of it, sitting cross-legged on the ground, was one of the Magi. From his mouth came the endless, mournful wail of the chant.

Cyrus stared for a few seconds then turned back to the boy. To his surprise, the lad's face was split by a wide grin. He raised two fingers to his head and tapped it. "Mad!" he mouthed. "Mad Magi!"

They continued until the shape of Gova Hall loomed out of the darkness ahead. The boy led them stealthily along the nearest side as far as the broad entrance. Here he stood and listened for a moment before pulling open the right-hand door. Then he slipped inside, beckoning them to follow.

The interior smelt of dried flowers. At the far end, raised on a wooden stand carved with symbols of the sun, a single candle burned. Its yellow light shimmered eerily across the crude images on the walls. The boy went down on his knees and, just below where Roxanne had seen the enamel notice with faded writing on it, began scrabbling around on the floor. Taja and Cyrus stared in astonishment as, very slowly and carefully, he raised a hinged concrete panel to reveal a dark hole beneath it.

The boy pointed to the opening. "Go on!"

Taja, who was nearer to the hole than Cyrus, hesitated. "Is it some sort of cell, a prison?"

The boy shook his head. "Prison? Don't be daft, lady! It's a tunnel!"

Taja shrugged and lowered herself into the opening. Cyrus

indicated to the boy to go next. He was sure the lad was honest, but all the same…Didn't the Children of Gova get rid of people by burying them alive? They may even have disposed of Roxanne in this very pit.

The boy shook his head. "You're the important one, mister. I'll shut the door after me."

"No. Sorry, boy. To be on the safe side, you go in front of me." When Cyrus folded his arms to show he meant what he said, the boy took a step towards the hole.

Before either of them realised what was happening, a tall figure sprang out from behind Cyrus and grabbed the boy by the shoulder. It was Ozlam!

"Stop, my child!" he ordered in a furious whisper. "This is a terrible heresy you commit! Oh my dear child, you have betrayed me and the secrets of the Great Gova!"

The boy struggled to free himself. "Get off me, Ozlam! I ain't your child! And I hate you and I hate your stupid Gova!"

The exchange lit up the darkened landscape of Cyrus' mind like a flash of summer lightning. Two things became clear immediately. Whoever he was, the boy was on their side; and Ozlam knew about the tunnel but wanted to keep it a secret. Why else would he whisper instead of calling for help?

The boy's pitiful remarks stirred Cyrus into action. He launched himself at Ozlam, wrenching his hands off the child and pushing him heavily backwards. The High Father recovered his balance and felt for something inside the folds of his robe.

"No weapons, eh?" mocked Cyrus as the bully drew out a glimmering blade.

The man's mouth arched into an unholy sneer. "Only for killing heretical and ungrateful vermin!"

Battle experience had taught Cyrus how to sum up an opponent in an instant. This one, he realised, was neither brave nor a fighter. Muttering over his shoulder, "Get in the tunnel, boy!" he advanced across the hall. After all he had been through, he finally had a chance to express his pent up fury in action.

Ozlam was slashing at the air in a futile effort at intimidation when Cyrus' foot slammed into his hand. The knife spun in a broad arc and clattered to the floor. The kick was instantly followed by a deft combination of punches. The first hammered into Ozlam's jaw, jerking his head backwards. The second thudded into his stomach, emptying the air from his lungs and folding him up like a penknife.

The final blow, delivered with the side of the hand, cracked into the back of Ozlam's neck. Without a sound, he sank senseless to the floor. Moments later, Cyrus and the boy had climbed through the hatchway, closed the trapdoor after them and were fumbling their way along the cobweb-tangled walls of the tunnel. They had gone no more than a couple of hundred paces before the boy stopped, took an object from a ledge and handed it to Cyrus. Feeling with his fingers in the blackness, he recognized the familiar outline immediately. His spear! The lad had not only rescued them – he had managed to save their weapons, too. He really was a most extraordinary character!

With Taja leading the way, they edged along the musty-smelling passage for a considerable distance. Every now and again Cyrus paused to listen for the sound of pursuit. Nothing.

Cyrus wondered how Ozlam was explaining his injuries, and the disappearance of his prisoners and one of his precious boys. Even he would find it difficult to lie his way out of that one.

The tunnel's exit was ingenious. Over the last one hundred paces the passage sloped steeply upwards until it came to a halt at the foot of an iron-runged ladder. This rose inside a tall, vertical shaft closed at the top by a heavy trapdoor. Pushing his way through and closing it behind him, Cyrus found himself on a platform high up in a tree made of fibreglass and concrete. The model was so well built that despite a century's weathering, it remained almost indistinguishable from the natural trees around it.

Holding onto a rope handrail that led to the broad bough of an adjacent oak, Cyrus, Taja and the boy climbed into its branches and slithered down the trunk to the ground. Their young guide then confirmed what Cyrus and Taja already suspected: they were well beyond the murderous perimeter of the Gova settlement. When they had thanked him repeatedly for saving them, they searched out a sheltered hollow, checked it for snakes and lay down to rest.

Before going to sleep, the Tallins insisted that their new friend explain what was going on. The boy's story, told simply and without self-glorification, sparkled with intelligence, kindness and remarkable courage. It also brought a smile to Cyrus' face and allowed him to close his eyes with a glimmer of hope in his bruised heart.

Timur, too, had been the recipient of startling news from the mouth of a youngster. Its bearer was the favoured message-carrier whom the Malik had singled out as a possible heir apparent.

"Zeds!" gasped the young man, struggling for breath after running halfway down the hill in search of his master. "Giv seen Zeds!"

Timur's brow furrowed like dirty snow. Zeds? Of course the fool could see Zeds! "What Zeds?" he asked, restraining himself from striking the youth for his stupidity.

"Enemy Zeds, Malik! Not Grozny!"

The creases on Timur's brow deepened. Interference from another Zed tribe was the last thing he needed. It was difficult enough keeping his numbheaded warriors in some sort of line when there were no distractions. If they had to contend with other Zeds as well, it would be beyond even his ferocious powers of control. He needed detail.

"Where are these Zeds, Giv? Point!"

"Er, leff!" cried Giv proudly, sticking out the correct arm like a salute in the direction of the shallow valley below.

At least they're not behind us, thought Timur. "Good, Giv. You have the makings of a mind. Now, see if you can use it again. This might not be easy, but how many are there?"

The youth's grin was replaced by a pained expression that betrayed his difficulty in grasping the question. Like all common Zeds, he was unable to count.

Timur tried again. "How many bad Zeds?" He held up three long white fingers. "This many?"

Giv shook his head. "No, Malik. More bad Zeds." He held

up both his hands with all the fingers outstretched. "Hundred!"

"Make up your mind, ratvomit!" screeched Timur, whose patience was fraying rapidly as the potential danger of the situation became apparent. "Ten fingers are not a hundred!" He held up his own hands, the digits extended like asparagus sticks. "This is ten. Got it, leadhead? Ten."

"Giv see ten bad Zeds over leff," the lad explained carefully, pointing again towards the river.

Timur nodded. "Learning fast, Giv. Well, let's see what can be done about them."

When Timur reached the top of the hill from which Giv had come, he found his men in a state of high excitement. Delighted by the prospect of action, they were jumping about, punching each other and brandishing their weapons in the air. Their leader realised at once that he wouldn't be able to deny their animal craving for action. He peered down the slope. Yes, Giv was almost right. Some fifteen hundred paces away was a small group of men – he could see nine – who appeared to be hurrying away from him. Their peculiar assortment of weapons and lack of clothing marked them as Zeds.

"Want go kill!" grunted a tall man with a dark hole where his left eye had been. "Zeds want go kill!"

"Listen to me!" yelled Timur. "Listen!" The men gradually fell silent. "You men here, only you may go and kill those Zeds! Just you! Repeat!"

"Just you!" echoed the mob. Misunderstanding the command, three or four warriors started to move.

"Stop!" screamed Timur. "Batbrains! Wait for the orders of

your Malik. Giv, you tell the men on the left, and Jamshid, you tell the men on the right" – to make sure he was understood, he indicated both directions as he spoke – "that they must stay in the line. Understand? Stay in the line! Repeat!"

"Stay in the line," they chorused eagerly.

"Brilliant! Now go!"

As Giv and Captain Jamshid ran off, Timur turned once again to the men clustered around him. "Now, you brainless bloodshedders, go and get those Zeds! Ready…charge!"

With a medley of savage war cries, the band of some forty Zed warriors rushed madly down the hill. It was at this point that Timur's strategy collapsed. The Zeds at the bottom of the hill, fleeing from what was clearly a much larger force, broke into a run and veered away to the right. This brought them within sight of another group of Timur's men. Before Jamshid arrived with orders to stay put, this force of about forty abandoned their positions and joined the furious charge of their confederates.

Seeing what was about to descend on them, the targeted Zeds hesitated for a few seconds then doubled back to Timur's left. The same pattern of indiscipline was repeated on this flank. Without waiting for orders, the frenzied warriors screamed with delight at the sight of potential victims and hurtled down the slope after them. By now well over one hundred men – nearly all the Grozny Zeds' military force – were careering out of control in pursuit of a rapidly retreating enemy.

Timur groaned. For the moment there was nothing he could do as most of his men were already out of earshot. It would probably take them the rest of the day to catch their prey, kill it and bring what was left of the bodies back to him. When they did so, however, someone was going to pay for this indiscipline. Pay a very painful price indeed.

Cyrus was dreaming. He was lying on soft grass back in Della Tallis. Ozlam was talking to Roxanne. He leaned across and whispered something in her ear. She laughed, tossing back her hair to reveal the Zed tattoo. The High Father opened his mouth in a joyless smile and ran his finger over the cruel scar. When she did not object, he took her hand, raised her from the ground and started to lead her away.

"No! Roxy! Don't go! Please don't go!" It was dream-speech. Cyrus didn't know whether he was really talking or not.

"I won't go again, Cy."

Again? What did that mean? Floating between sleeping and waking, Cyrus opened his eyes. Ozlam had gone, but not Roxanne...Roxanne? He was suddenly wide awake.

Memories of the previous night slipped into focus: the boy, the musty tunnel, the hollow where they had gone to sleep. He remembered, too, what the boy had told them. He was sure Roxanne had managed to get away...

Cyrus didn't know whether to laugh or cry. He stood up and walked slowly over to where she was standing beside the boy. This was a greater miracle than anything Gova was supposed to have done. Wrapping his arms around the woman who had changed the purpose and meaning of his life, he held her to him. "Oh, Roxy!" he whispered, his face buried in her thick dark hair. "Oh, Roxy, I really do – "

141

"How sweet! How childishly, pathetically sweet!" Taja's voice was thick with more than sarcasm. "I thought we were on a mission to find the Soterion, Cyrus, not a lover."

Keeping hold of Roxanne's hand, Cyrus took a step back. "Listen, Taja. We are in the middle of a crucial and very difficult operation. It has been painful and will probably get worse – "

"So we must concentrate on the task in hand and not let personal feelings get in the way." Taja's eyes were black and furious.

"Precisely, Taja," replied Cyrus slowly, meeting her gaze and holding it. "We must not let personal feelings get in the way."

It was the boy who brought the exchange to a halt. "Excuse me," he interrupted, "I don't know nothing about this personal feelings stuff, but shouldn't we be getting on with something else?"

Roxanne put an arm round his thin shoulders. "Thank you for reminding us, Sammy. But I think there's a bit of explaining to do first, don't you?"

The emergency tunnel, which ran from the hall to the concrete tree over a thousand paces away, had been built into the structure of the Gova settlement at the same time as the electric fence. Its purpose was to allow entry and exit if the gates malfunctioned. The position of the hatch in the hall was indicated by an enamel sign – the one Roxanne had started reading. When Ozlam noticed her doing this, it gave him another reason to get rid of her: she knew his secret.

As literacy had died out soon after the community's

foundation, the sign had lost its meaning. Furthermore, as the tunnel was never used and the floor of the hall became covered with thick layers of dust, within thirty years the very existence of the escape route was forgotten.

It had been rediscovered by the literate refugee Constants who, when sheltering among the Children of Gova, had mocked their unscientific cult. Frinaspa, the High Father of the time, had ordered the iconoclasts' swift burial for heresy and kept the knowledge of the tunnel to himself. He passed it on only to his successor.

The High Fathers who followed found the secret extremely useful. To stop anyone abandoning the settlement, they came up with the practice of throwing the insulation from the handles over the fence. This left the levers as deadly as the surrounding wire and struts. The Fathers, or occasionally a trusted Magus, then used the tunnel to sneak out under the cover of darkness to recover the insulation. Its restoration, they explained, was one of Gova's miracles.

This dishonest ritual continued unchanged until the time of Ozlam's predecessor, Torpekai. Both he and Ozlam shared the same unpleasant characteristics: they were cowards and strongly disliked women. Neither man fathered children. Instead, they surrounded themselves with a group of favoured boys whom they educated – as Taja had correctly guessed – to be the future Magi. The secret of the tunnel was revealed to one of these lads so that he, and not the High Father or a Magus, ran the risk of going beyond the fence to collect the insulation. Ozlam's great mistake was in his choice of boy.

The lad's full name was Sammy Songova, although he never referred to himself as that. "Songova" was the surname given to all future Magi – and he hated it. Fearless, bright, lively and scrupulously honest, Sammy was a born rebel.

Although the "electricity heresy" of twenty-eight years previously had been wiped out, some of the Children still felt their leaders were not being quite straight with them. A few even went so far as secretly to question the whole Gova idea. It was only a story, they said, invented to maintain the tyrannical overlordship of the High Father and the Magi. Among these dissenters were Sammy and his young friends, the self-named "No-Goves".

When Sammy heard of Ozlam's order to execute the newly arrived Constant lady with the kindly eyes, he determined to help her – and free himself at the same time. His aim was to lead her and her friends out on the same night. So they would not be at the mercy of Zeds beyond the fence, he had not destroyed their weapons, as Ozlam had commanded, but hidden them in the tunnel and burned some old wooden posts as substitutes.

Sammy got his timing wrong. While he was sliding back the bolt on the door of Roxanne's prison, he heard someone approaching. It was a Magus on his way to take over the night-time chant. As Sammy was backing away from the door, the man looked at him suspiciously: community rules said everyone had to stay in their dormitories from dusk to dawn. Fortunately, the Magus passed by without comment. He must have assumed that Sammy, Ozlam's favourite, was on his way to see him.

"I can imagine how you felt, Sammy," said Roxanne, "when

you came back after the man had gone and discovered the bolt of my prison closed again and me missing!"

The boy grinned. "I tell you, lady, I thought maybe you'd gone up in smoke! But I had a sneaky look at the trapdoor in the hall. The dirt around it had been moved so I knew someone had opened it. Smart lady, I thought to myself. She's got away alright."

Cyrus glanced across at Taja. While she was listening to the story as keenly as himself, it was clear from her disappointed expression she found it painful. A short while ago, although a captive, she had been alone with him. Now Roxanne was back, her hopes had been dashed once more. But she could wait, she told herself. Her time may yet come.

As soon as the coast was clear, Roxanne was explaining, she had let herself out of the prison chamber and made a quick plan of action. The first move was to rescue Corby, whose whining she had heard over the sound of the chanting. That done, she planned to use the dog to help her find Cyrus, Taja and Navid. She had not gone more than five steps before she realised the idea wouldn't work: Corby's loud snuffling would wake the whole settlement in no time.

Reluctantly, she decided it was best to leave immediately – assuming that the tunnel was still intact and led somewhere safe – and return the next day to collect the others. She reckoned she could work out where they were by watching the settlement during daylight.

Roxanne looked at Cyrus rather sheepishly. "No, I didn't abandon you, Cy. I simply reckoned it was better to get out than be caught. You see, I thought I was the only one who knew about the tunnel.

"The plan didn't work, anyway. When I got up here, I found the tree surrounded by Zeds." She frowned. "They were obviously looking for us, probably heading for that bridge I mentioned. I went back into the tunnel, where I'd left Corby, and the two of us hid there all day. We were famished and thirsty. Poor Corby's tongue was hanging out so far I thought it would drop off!"

Roxanne stooped and patted the dog's broad flank. "When the Zeds had gone, I hauled him up to the tunnel entrance by his collar. Almost strangled you, didn't I?" she said playfully, scratching the top of his head. "Sorry, old thing, but it was worth it, wasn't it?"

The creature looked up at her with huge eyes as if to say, "Well, I suppose so."

"The moment I got him on the ground, he shot off to find water, just as he did when he sniffed out that stream after the ambush."

The rest of the tale was soon told. Refreshed with water from a muddy hollow and her hunger satisfied with wild fruits, Roxanne lay down to sleep with Corby at her side. Shortly before dawn, she was woken by his damp nose pushing against her face. He seemed to want to go somewhere. At first light, Roxanne let him have his way and followed him to the hollow where she found Cyrus, Taja and Sammy fast asleep.

The whole story now came together. Once it was discovered that Roxanne and Corby had vanished, rumours began to circulate among the Children of Gova. The Magus who had bumped into Sammy in the middle of the night told others what he had seen. By mid-morning, the boy felt people were watching him wherever he went. He now needed to free the remaining Constants and get away himself.

"So, here we all are," Sammy concluded cheerily. "I'll miss my mates, sure. But I tell you, anything's better than being stuck in that wicked place. That Ozlam, he's really nasty, he is."

"I'm sure he is, Sammy," said Cyrus, "and I can't tell you how grateful we are for what you have done. However, we mustn't forget that poor Navid, my Defender companion, is still inside."

"It was his choice," cut in Taja. The edge had returned to her voice, Cyrus noted. What extraordinary self-control she had! She sounded tougher, more determined than ever.

"Yes, but he made that choice when he thought the mission was over and Corby was dead. If he could see us now – and Corby – I bet he'd want to come back."

Taja shrugged. "Maybe. But there's nothing we can do about it."

"Excuse me, lady," interrupted Sammy, "there is something. I'll go and get him!"

A heated conversation followed, but in the end Sammy had his way. He knew where Navid was and assured them he could smuggle him out. As soon as it was dark, he said goodbye to his new friends and re-entered the tunnel. As proof to Navid that his companions and his beloved Corby were alive and well, in his pocket he carried the dog's leather collar and a ring Cyrus had inherited from his father.

Sammy was gone half the night. When he reappeared, followed by a rather guilty-looking Navid, even Taja allowed herself to smile. Roxanne embraced Sammy and called him a hero. Cyrus shook his friend warmly by the hand and assured him he had no need to apologise for what had gone on. Not to miss out on the rejoicing, Corby ran around licking every hand within reach. By the time all the laughing, congratulating and story-swapping had finished, dawn was already breaking. Taking up their weapons, the Constants set off once more in the direction of the River No-Man.

Having lost several days, the mission was eager to move quickly. Knowing that Timur and his Zeds were somewhere ahead, apparently going the same way, they proceeded with extreme caution. They were surprised, therefore, when towards evening on the third day they arrived at the ruined bridge on the banks of the No-Man without having seen or heard anything of the enemy.

As Timur had feared, it had taken his warriors the better part of a day to chase down their enemy. The six slower runners were swiftly overhauled and hacked to death. The remaining three proved harder to catch. Having run in a group for a few thousand paces, they separated and headed off in different directions. This led to a ferocious argument among the pursuers, who eventually divided themselves into three groups. They did not corner the last man until nightfall. As was their custom, he was not slaughtered, as the others had been, but bound and saved for the grizzly ritual of the spit.

Timur had left his position on the hill in order to follow his undisciplined men and save time. That was why, when the Constants skirted round the same hill a day later, they came across nothing to suggest that the Grozny Zeds had ever been there.

The advance of the Grozny Zeds was further slowed by victory celebrations, including the ceremonial spit feast, and the whipping and mutilation of those he held responsible for leaving their positions without his permission. The fighting men also had to wait for the rest of the tribe – the dogs, children, breeding slaves and other menials – to catch them up. Thus two days had passed before Timur re-established his line and resumed sweeping across the countryside between himself and the river.

After a brief discussion, Cyrus, Roxanne, Taja, Navid and Sammy decided to cross the No-Man that evening. They would be safer on the other side, they reasoned, because the Zed hunting dogs wouldn't be able to negotiate ten paces of unsupported rusty rail and would have to be swung across the gap in some sort of sling. Keen to make up for what he had done in the Gova community, Navid volunteered to go first. He had a good sense of balance, he assured them, and could walk along a single line without difficulty.

The river bank was very still. There was no breeze and the only sounds were the gentle swirl of the grey-green waters far below the bridge and the occasional harsh cry of a rook. The iron walkway on the first span of the bridge remained intact and Navid's footsteps sounded unnaturally loud as he made his way cautiously across it.

On reaching the end of the solid platform, he stopped and looked down. "Hey!" he called. "Someone's knocked a bit off here. Marks are new. Looks like they've been trying to smash it up."

Cyrus glanced around, sensing danger. The silence was ominous. "Careful, Nav!" he shouted. "Don't carry on unless you're absolutely certain it's OK."

"No problem, Cy. Here we go!"

Navid stepped onto the steel rail and stood there for a few seconds, gathering himself. As he began to inch forward, a loud twang echoed from the opposite bank. A moment later, something clanged onto the ironwork behind him.

"Eh? What's that?" Navid paused, swaying gently over the abyss.

Sammy pointed across the river. "Look! There's a bloke on the other side!"

"Navid!" screamed Cyrus. "Get back!"

A second arrow rattled against the crumbling ironwork. Navid jumped off the rail and ran back down the walkway to the safety of the bank. "So what do we do now?" he panted.

"OK, we stay here and keep an eye on the bridge to make sure whoever's over there doesn't sneak up on us when it gets dark," said Cyrus. "We can decide on our next move in the morning."

"Nice idea, Cyrus," said Taja calmly, "but I think you'll find the morning will be too late. Listen!"

Through the still of the evening came the sound they had

all been dreading. The terrifying baying of hounds. Timur had them cornered, precisely as he had planned: as flies in a jar, they were trapped.

8
The Crossing

Sammy looked at Taja. "What's that noise then, Taj?"

Taja pretended not to hear him. No one had ever called her anything but "Taja" before and she was not going to let a youngster start now, however grateful she was to him for getting her out of the Gova settlement.

"It's dogs," explained Navid.

"Oh! Like Corby, you mean?"

"No, not really. The ones making that racket are hunting dogs. They're known as 'hounds'. They chase animals and kill them. Except this time it's us they're after, not something to eat like rabbits or deer."

Roxanne gave him an uneasy look. Though the explanation was neat, in one appalling respect it wasn't quite true – though this was hardly the time to enlighten him. Navid's words raised another issue, too. It struck her that Timur, instead of using the dogs to hunt her, might have chosen to let them track her and lead him to the Soterion. Whichever course he had decided on, the mission had to throw him off their scent. That meant crossing the river.

During the exchange between Navid and Sammy, Cyrus had been assessing their position and had come to the same conclusion as Roxanne. The barking was yet some way off: he estimated it would be almost dark by the time the Zeds reached the river. So what to do? There was no going back or trying to sneak off down the bank; judging by the direction of the din, their pursuers were closing in from all sides. That left only one option. They had to force their way across the bridge, whatever the cost.

Cyrus clapped his hands for attention. "Decision time! We've got to find a way of getting to the opposite bank – there's no way we can stand and fight the whole of the Grozny."

"I've never done any fighting," said Sammy anxiously. "What's it like?"

Navid gave a low grunt. "It's OK if you win, Sammy – "

"Exactly," interrupted Cyrus, keen to get on with things. "We fight only if we have to and when we've got a chance of winning. If we give battle here, we'll be completely outnumbered; however good we are, we'll be hacked to pieces or, worse still, taken prisoner."

Roxanne, who had been staring absent-mindedly at the murky river, nodded vehemently. She would rather throw herself into the crocodile-infested No-Man than fall into Timur's hands again.

"I've been thinking about what happened when Navid tried to cross," Cyrus continued. "We saw only one person shooting at him, yes?"

There was general agreement on this. "OK. The trouble is, he's unlikely to be alone. Someone's planned this and, from what Roxanne's told us, there's only one Zed who could do that. Timur. I can't believe Timur would have sent just one man to hold the bridge against us."

"One, two, three...I don't care," said Navid. "If we stand here nattering we'll never even find out. Whatever you say, Cy, I'm going to have another go."

All he needed, he went on, was for Taja to cover him while he was on the rail. Positioning herself on the bridge behind him, the opposite bank would be within range. Once on the other side, he was confident of being able to take care of a Zed or two.

"And after that?" queried Taja. "Assuming, of course, that the Grozny haven't arrived by then and skewered the rest of us."

Picking up on Navid's plan, Cyrus suggested that once his friend was across and confronting whoever had shot at him, he'd be able to get over unopposed to help. While this was going on, Roxanne and Sammy should cut down a pole to use as a handrail.

"What about Corby?" asked Sammy, patting his new friend on the head. "He won't be able to hold on to a bit of wood with them paw things he's got, will he?"

They agreed to try the Navid-Cyrus attack, and if it worked, they would make some sort of hammock out of their clothes and pass the dog across using the rail. It was not a particularly clever or clear idea and, if they were honest, none of them was sure it would work. As none of them came up with anything better, however, they had no choice but to give it a go.

The mission's second contrivance for getting safely across the river was altogether more ingenious. It came from Roxanne. As Navid was getting ready to climb onto the bridge a second time, she called for him to wait a moment. Then, to the astonishment and even slight embarrassment of her friends, she peeled off her loose-fitting dress and handed it to him.

"Here, Navid," she said calmly, "take this and put it on."

Navid's face fell. "It's alright," she explained. "It may look a bit odd, but listen, I'll explain what we'll do."

Captain Jumshid was feeling rather pleased with himself. True, the bridge was still standing – his blows had little impact on the ironwork and he had been unable to think of any other way of bringing the structure down. Nevertheless, as the Malik had ordered, he had prevented the Constants from crossing. If they tried in the dark, all he would have to do was climb back onto the bridge and position himself on the edge of the gap between the spans. From there it would be easy to push into the river anyone advancing towards him. That would almost certainly not be necessary: the baying of Grozny hounds was getting closer with every moment that passed.

The difficulty of balancing on a single rail for some ten paces over a lethal river had also given Jumshid a plausible explanation for Sheza's absence. He would tell Timur that the young man had simply lost his balance and tumbled into the No-Man. It wasn't so far from the truth, either.

"Good man, Jumshid!" the Captain said quietly to himself, puffing out his chest and imitating the high-pitched voice of his master. "You not ratbrain! No, you now Captain Cleverman!"

Grinning at his own success, Jumshid looked out across the bridge from his hiding place. Daylight was fading fast and he could now barely make out the dim shapes of the Constants moving around on the opposite bank. What a lovely choice they had! Fall into the hands of the mighty Malik, jump into the No-Man and be eaten alive, or be shot by him…

Wait a moment! Another one of them was going to attempt the crossing. As Jumshid watched, a figure stepped up onto the bridge and advanced along the iron footpath. He was bigger than the last one, much bigger.

The Captain's eyes widened in amazement as the shape lurched awkwardly forward. It was enormous – a giant! Although not especially tall, the monster man was as broad as an oak, with arms like a horse's thigh. Jumshid placed an arrow against the string of his bow. The bigger the target, he told himself, the easier it was to hit.

As his enemy reached the end of the walkway, Jumshid took a few steps down the bank to get a better aim. Something whizzed past his left ear. Eh? There was another figure, a much smaller one, shooting at him from the bridge. He slipped behind an iron girder and peered round.

The giant was now halfway across the gap, edging in his direction. He couldn't miss. Jumshid stepped out from his hiding place, pulled back his bow, took careful aim and let the arrow fly.

Thwack! The sound of the metal-tipped missile striking its target echoed dully across the river and a flock of startled ducks rose squawking into the heavy evening air. Jumshid stared in astonishment. He had hit his target alright – there was his arrow sticking out of the giant's chest like a wayward rib. And yet… The monster was still moving! True, it had swayed a little when the arrow struck, but it had regained its balance and resumed its ungainly progress.

Thwack! A second arrow buried its shaft in the giant's chest beside the first. Once again the swollen creature swayed before righting itself and moving on. By the time Navid – for it was indeed he – set foot on the secure walkway on the far end of the bridge, no fewer than five wooden shafts projected from his massive trunk.

"See!" he roared, seizing each arrow in turn and breaking it in half, "Your puny weapons cannot harm me. Prepare to die, Zed!"

Jumshid, like all his kind, scarcely knew the meaning of fear. But this thing, this bellowing giant, unnerved him. If it was not killed by arrows, what hope had he? Should he stand his ground or flee?

The indecision cost the captain his miserable life. Unsure what to do as Navid lumbered towards him, he froze. The fight, such as it was, ended with a single blow of the Constant's mighty axe.

Unable to bend over because of his girth, the victor knelt and seized something from the dust at his feet. He rose again, swung it round a few times, then hurled it far into the grey-black waters of the No-Man. The head of Captain Jumshid sank like a rock.

Cyrus arrived at his friend's side in time to help him push the decapitated body into the river. They quickly scoured the surrounding scrub to confirm that the Zed had indeed been acting alone and called back to the others that it was safe. Navid then pulled off Roxanne's rough woollen dress and unwrapped the protective layers of bark and thick leaves packed between it and his own tunic.

Meanwhile, Roxanne and Taja had cut a long pole from a tree and pushed it across the gap to act as a handrail. As they jammed their end firmly between two intersecting girders, Cyrus used a length of twisted creeper to secure his end to a rusty upright.

Taja went first, holding firmly to the pole to keep her balance. Then Roxanne grasped Sammy's hand and guided him safely across. As she neared them, Cyrus and Navid looked away. Although not prudish, the Tallins prided themselves on their sense of respect: they were not shocked by Roxanne's bare chest but felt it would have been bad manners to stare too obviously at so handsome a woman wearing only a pair of coarse linen breeches.

Shouting to Corby to stay where he was, Navid stepped onto the rail. "Soon have you over, old boy," he called. The dog was obviously worried. His ears pricked and he whined, looking anxiously behind him. Seconds later, when Navid was about halfway across, the source of his faithful companion's anxiety came bursting over the top of the bank and howling down towards the river. The Grozny Zeds and their hounds had found their quarry – and Corby was stuck on the wrong side of the gap.

What occurred next would become a legend in Constant folklore. Seeing the danger to his master and his friends, Corby ran to the end of the bridge and stood there snarling, defying anyone to pass. Had he remained there, he would certainly have been killed.

Navid, perched on a narrow rail above the dark waters, made a swift calculation. If he went forward to fight beside his dog, he too would die. At best, he might delay the assault on the crossing by a moment or two. On the other hand, if he retreated, there was a chance…

Deftly keeping his footing, Navid swivelled round and hurried back to the metal footpath on the far end of the bridge. By now the leading Zeds, struggling to keep up with their straining hounds, had almost made it onto the bridge themselves. One or two were already bending forward to unleash their animals. Navid raised his fingers to his mouth and gave a long, shrill whistle. "Here, Corby!" he yelled. "Come here, boy! Run!"

For an instant the dog paused, unsure whether to obey his instinct or his master. Loyalty won. Turning, he bounded down the bridge. Behind him, half a dozen Zed dogs, now freed from their handlers, set off in pursuit.

Corby had the advantage of knowing what lay ahead. As he approached the opening, he seemed to measure his pace like a long jumper. When his nose was level with the end of the path, he crouched like a lion and sprang.

No human could have cleared that dreadful gap and probably no other dog. Rising like a stupendous bird, Corby's dark shape arced upwards against the evening sky. For a split second, it hung there before falling in a steepening curve towards the distant walkway.

Somewhere in the twilit background, Sammy cried out, "Go, Corby! Go!"

The leap was mighty, yet not quite sufficient. The dog's broad head, shoulders and front paws reached the safety of the other side, but his rear legs and the bulk of his heavy body were left dangling in mid-air. Very slowly, claws scrabbling desperately for a grip on the slippery metal, Corby began to slide backwards into the void.

Navid saved him. Now free of his cumbersome padding, he darted forward and grabbed his loyal companion by the collar. Sammy was soon kneeling next to him and the two of them hauled the quivering creature to safety.

The Zed hounds were less fortunate. Ignorant of the missing span, they hurtled along the iron platform until it suddenly disappeared beneath their feet. Six animals that Timur could ill afford to lose spun slowly in the thick air and splashed into the black water below. Like all dogs, the creatures swam instinctively – but the skill was of little use. The waiting crocodiles, their appetites whetted by the corpse of Jumshid and alerted by the noise from the bridge, seized the hounds in their merciless jaws and dragged them down into the oily depths.

By this time, Timur had appeared on the bank above the river. Abandoning his canopy and escort, he had joined in the chase himself to ensure that Roxanne was taken alive. He speedily assessed the situation. Sheza and Jumshid had plainly failed him; he would deal with them later – if they were still alive. At least he now knew exactly where the Constants were and their numbers. Two men, two women, a dog and what looked like a boy. Hmm. They really shouldn't be that much of a problem.

The first thing was to get across the bridge. As it would be impossible to balance on a single railway line and fight at the same time, the pathway needed to be broader. The obvious way to do that was to lay pieces of wood across the tracks. Immediately, orders went out for his men not to attack across the lines in the dark but to cut logs three paces long and pile them up at the entrance to the bridge ready for an attack in the morning. The plan was a good one. It was never put into operation, however, because by dawn the third span of the bridge, like the central one, had disappeared. With it had gone the rails, the last link across the No-Man. The river had become impassable.

While Navid and Sammy were busy saving Corby, the others had gathered armfuls of dry sticks and grass from the bank and laid them on the wooden beams beneath the rails on their side of the bridge. Their intention had been simply to build a fire in order to hold up the Zeds and give the mission time to get away. It was soon clear, once the flames had taken hold of the remaining wood on which the rails rested, that the conflagration would do more than delay the Grozny. Working by the light of the fire, the Constants fed the blaze with everything combustible they could lay their hands on. As the inferno soared higher and higher, the old iron, weakened by decades of rust, began to twist and groan in the extreme heat. Once-mighty girders buckled like green twigs. Below them, the crumbling brickwork of the pier cracked and splintered.

Finally, warned by a cry from Navid, the Constants dashed back to the bank in time to see an entire section of the bridge, flaming and roaring like a gigantic torch, crash hissing into the water. Their cheers of delight carried across the river to the opposite bank. Hearing it, Timur bit his bottom lip with such fury that blood dripped from his chin onto the dirt at his feet.

The days that followed the crossing of the No-Man were the easiest of the entire mission. Freed from the worry of pursuing Grozny, the five Constants hurried in the direction of the noonday sun until, one afternoon, they reached the remains of a Long Dead highway that Roxanne identified from faded signs as number 24. It led, she remembered the Albans saying, all the way to the settlement where the mystical Soterion had been found.

Walking and talking amongst themselves for day after day, the five travellers learned much about each other. On the first morning, they listened fascinated as Roxanne explained where the idea of making protective clothing for Navid had come from. The inspiration, she explained with a laugh, was *Peter Pan*.

It was a really strange volume, she continued, because no one understood what it was for. In the opinion of most Yonne scholars, books were for passing on information, telling the reader things. That's what the *IKEA Catalogue* and the Third Book did. *Peter Pan* was weirdly different. It was a story about events that she was fairly sure had never happened – it even had a place in it called Neverland.

"You mean a sort of dreaming place?" asked Sammy, looking at Roxanne with a mixture of curiosity and admiration.

"I suppose so. A land where children fly and crocodiles swallow alarm clocks and there is a pirate with a hook where his hand had once been…"

"Hang on! Hang on! You've lost me, Roxanne. Kids can't fly, and what's an 'alarm clock' and a 'pirate' and how can a bloke have a hook instead of a hand?"

Roxanne smiled. After she had explained her padding idea, she said, she would tell Sammy the whole story of *Peter Pan* from beginning to end. She then recounted how Tootles, one of the Lost Boys, had shot a girl named Wendy thinking she was a bird. Everyone believed she was dead until it was discovered that the arrow had been prevented from entering her heart by a button she was wearing round her neck. For some reason Roxanne did not quite understand, the button, given to Wendy by the boy Peter, was known as a "kiss".

It was how the button protected Wendy from Tootles' arrow that gave Roxanne the idea of doing something similar for Navid.

He gave her a broad grin. "Worked, too. Thanks Peterpan, whoever you are. Bark and leaves instead of a button. Just as good. You should have seen that Zed's face! Mind you, Roxanne, lucky he didn't aim at my head."

"Wouldn't have mattered if he had," joked Cyrus. "I'd like to see the arrow that could get through your thick skull!" They all laughed, or rather four of them did. Taja managed only a wry smile.

"And when we gets to this Alba place," chipped in Sammy, "I reckons we should get you a new dress. One without holes in it. Gets a bit drafty on the inside bits when the wind's blowing, don't it?"

"No. Keeps me cool," said Roxanne, waggling a finger through one of the holes. "So Sammy, want to hear the story of Peter Pan?"

"That'd be great, Roxanne. Thanks. They didn't like stories back where I come from. It was all chanting and Gova-this and Gova-that. So tell me about this Peter bloke and Neverland and that man what had a hook."

The story lasted for much of the rest of the day. Roxanne, who could remember the text almost word for word, started by telling it only to Sammy; by the time she had finished, all four of her fellow travellers formed an enchanted audience. None of them had ever heard anything like it. The life of a Constant was hard and practical, with little time for fanciful tales.

When the story was over and Roxanne had done her best to answer the dozens of questions they asked, they made her promise to tell it again the next day. She in turn thanked them. Reciting the tale to complete strangers, she said, to people who knew nothing of the world of the Long Dead and had never heard a work of such magical imagination, she began to understand what *Peter Pan* was for.

Unlike the *IKEA Catalogue* and the Third Book of Yonne, it wasn't for anything very precise. It didn't contain information or instructions – at least, not directly – which meant it had only one purpose: it was for entertainment, for enjoyment, for fun!

The author wanted his story to bring smiles to people's faces.

"Worked OK with me," grinned Sammy. "So, d'you reckon there are more fun stories like that in this Soterion place, Roxanne?"

"I hope so, Sammy," she replied wistfully. "Yes, I really do hope so."

Before she fell asleep that night, Roxanne thought again about why Peter Pan might have been written. For amusement, yes, but perhaps it also had a secret message to do with children and adults? Maybe a book with a hero who never grew older meant it was good not to grow up, that children knew things their parents didn't? How odd! Like many aspects of the Long Dead world, it didn't make much sense to her at present. But she was sure it would one day, when they reached the Soterion...

Every day, for most of the morning, Cyrus continued with his education. Guided by Roxanne and writing with a lump of chalk on a piece of slate-like stone, he learned the letters of the alphabet and how to join them together into words. His spelling made her laugh. Nevertheless, as the days passed he read accurately more and more of the words she wrote down for him. "Zed" was easy, and he soon got the hang of "Cyrus", "Sammy" and "Taja", although he read the latter as "tiger", which made them both chuckle the first time he tried.

While all this was going on, the Mudir of the West Tower remained as enigmatic as on the day she had invited herself onto the mission. She rarely said much to anyone but Cyrus, choosing to walk alone at the back of the group seemingly lost in her own contemplations. She pulled her weight, shooting game for them to eat and taking her turn to stand watch at night; yet about the purpose of their mission, of finding the hidden vault and unlocking its secrets, she was curiously silent.

Once, falling in beside her as they wound their way up a rocky incline, Cyrus asked her what she thought about all day. She looked up at him with those deep black eyes and allowed herself a rare smile.

"There's no mystery, Cyrus," she said quietly. "Nothing's changed."

"I understand. But you don't still think Roxy – Roxanne – is in league with the Zeds, do you?"

She shrugged. "Who knows?"

"But you've seen for yourself what's happened. We all know that it was thanks to her that we got across the river. Why would she do that if she were working for Timur? Be sensible, Taja! Please give her a chance!"

"I am giving her a chance, Cyrus. Just be careful, that's all. Nothing's ever quite as it seems, you know. This is not Neverland and you are not Peter Pan! Be careful."

Cyrus said nothing. He was tempted to ask Roxanne to join them so that they could both explain to Taja, once and for all, that a Z-shaped tattoo did not indicate a Zed heart. The idea might work, he mused, and he was desperate to get the issue settled. But when he thought it through, he decided against it. If it came to a confrontation, someone would end up losing and the atmosphere in the group would be poisonous. Besides, Taja was less difficult now than she had been. Whenever Cyrus looked, he still found her watching with those same unblinking eyes. But she didn't say anything. When he and Roxanne laughed together and lay side by side at night, she remained silent. Waiting in the dark.

Timur sulked for three days after the destruction of the bridge. With no one daring to go near him, he mooched about on his own, staring into the river and throwing stones at the dozy crocodiles. Without Roxanne, his dream was finished. He would never find that Soterion and be able to unlock its secrets. He would never have all knowledge, as the Long Dead had done. He would never have all power. He would never be a god!

What made it worse, far worse, was that he had only himself to blame. Timur the Terrible, taken in by the flattery of a beautiful woman – how pathetic was that? He had to admit, though, she had been clever. All those fawning lies about how attractive she found him, and how she didn't need to be tied up because she would never leave him…Pah! It was too humiliating…

"Malik! Malik!" The familiar voice broke into Timur's thoughts. He turned abruptly ready to strike the fool who dared interrupt his brooding.

Giv had learned to read his master's capricious mind and stopped to kneel some distance away. "Good news, Great Malik!"

"And if it's not good, frogface, I'll cut your lying tongue in half!"

"Prisoner! Grozny capture prisoner!"

Timur's mood lightened. "Prisoner, Giv? What prisoner?"

"Constant man, Malik. Say he from place of Alba!"

Alba? Timur's black heart leapt. He had heard the name before, though he hadn't taken much notice of it at the time. It had come from the mouth of the batbrained woman captured at the same time as Roxanne. She was not only stupid but hysterically lamblivered – the cowardly cow had managed to kill herself before he had time to question her properly. But before she did so, he recalled, she had snivelled some pathetic drivel about her children back home – in Alba.

That was it, the vital clue had been within his grasp all along.

"Bring this Alban vermin in here immediately, Giv. I have a few questions for him."

As Giv scuttled off, the Malik brushed down his multi-coloured cloak and seated himself on the battered stainless steel chair that his bodyguard carried around for him. As long as his stupid warriors hadn't rendered the man from Alba speechless when they seized him, this should be very interesting indeed.

Timur was right. To begin with, the wretched prisoner said he wouldn't speak. Pain soon changed his mind. Bleeding, half blinded and with the bones in his left leg broken in two places, he confessed that he was indeed from Alba. After further torture, he admitted that, like two previous Alban missions, he had been on his way to Yonne. The Malik questioned him more intently, using a pair of pliers to inflict a particularly excruciating level of pain on the very tenderest parts of his anatomy. By the time the poor creature finally died, he had given the leader of the Grozny Zeds information that sent his spirits soaring and left him itching for action once more.

9
Outwitted

Timur's narrow lips stretched between his cheeks like a pair of mating snakes. When he smiled – always at his own delights or the misfortunes of others – the reptiles held their thin bodies in frozen congress and simply raised their heads and tails a fraction. The reason was not solely lack of mirth. The Malik disliked teeth. He avoided showing his own, scowled at the sight of them in others and was thrilled by any opportunity to knock them out. The phobia stemmed from the moment when, as a baby, he had been bitten on the arm by the mad dog that had just killed his mother.

On this occasion, as the Malik's mind pulsed with anticipated delights, the lip-vipers squirmed with unaccustomed vigour. What excellent news! She would not get away after all. Roxanne, the only woman who had ever managed to bewitch him into lowering his guard, was still within his grasp.

The Alban captive had surrendered a number of key pieces of information. He opened up when he heard Timur promise – on his mother's grave, no less – that he would end the torture and spare his life. Mother's grave! What fleece-hearted idiots these Constants were! His mother had no grave – her savaged body had been left in the open to rot. Even if she had been buried, what would the grave of a slave mean to him?

The Alban was half-dead anyway, and there was no way so dedicated a disciple of pain was going to forego the pleasure of finishing him off. Ah, the joy of torture! Arguably more fun than impregnating the breeding slaves, and certainly longer-lasting.

Timur's victim had been a member of the third Alban mission trying to make contact with a community of literate Constants. There had been four in the party originally, two men and two women. Having lost their way soon after departure, they had wandered through the semi-arid scrub for days looking for the remains of a highway. The two women had died of dysentery and the other man had fallen victim to a snake bite. The survivor had thought himself the fortunate one – until he fell into the hands of Timur.

Many seasons ago, he said, the Albans had found a cave sealed with a steel door dating from the time of the Long Dead. On it were words and a symbol believed to confirm that what lay within was the fabled Soterion: the place where the knowledge of the Long Dead was stored. Unable to read the instructions on how to enter the cave, the Alban Majlis had sent a series of missions to find literate Constants to assist them.

The first mission had vanished without trace, the prisoner declared.

"Not quite without trace," grimaced Timur. When his victim

tried to ask what that meant, he was silenced by a crushing blow to the groin that left him unable to speak for the rest of the morning.

Further questioning revealed that three surviving members of a second, larger mission had returned home when ten of their colleagues were swept to their deaths by a flash flood while trying to cross the upper reaches of the No-Man.

The Alban's revelations filled the gaps in Timur's understanding left by Roxanne's escape. But it was what the man admitted when told his torment would end that had his torturer's twisted mind writhing with glee. The failure of two missions had produced a bitter rift among the citizens of Alba, he learned. The majority felt they should continue to try to contact literate Constants, even if it meant sending out a hundred missions. Their opponents, led by a woman named Padmar, argued for a different tactic. Since their own missions were ill-suited to the hostile environment between themselves and Yonne, she suggested, couldn't they employ someone better able to cope with the conditions? Why not get a Zed to do the job? All they had to do was pay a powerful barbarian warrior to locate and capture a literate Constant and bring them back to Alba.

The proposal caused uproar. Chima, the Alban Emir, said it went against every principle they had ever held. She hardly had to remind them that Zeds were despicable savages. If invited to bring in one Constant, they would probably kill fifty in the process. They were not to be trusted, either. It would be sheer folly to jeopardise their impregnable mountain stronghold by inviting a single one of them inside the walls for negotiation. Padmar's plan was a non-starter, the Emir insisted. The great majority of her fellow officers agreed with her.

But Padmar was an obstinate, forceful woman. When she persevered with her argument, Chima eventually agreed a compromise. A third mission would be sent out. If that too failed, then the subject might be raised again. Until that time, any talk of employing a Zed was forbidden.

All this Timur extracted from the dying prisoner. It was invaluable intelligence. To use it to his advantage, he had to do two things. First, let the Albans know that their third mission had failed. Second, guarantee that the idea of employing a Zed was adopted. To do that, this woman Padmar needed a nice, friendly, civilised Zed to present as evidence that some barbarians might be trusted.

Now, who might that Zed be? Timur wrapped his long arms around his body and hugged himself gleefully. The answer was obvious. In fact, he held it in his very hands.

Timur had to act fast – and in secret. There was no point in blundering over to Alba, assuming he could find the place, with the whole Grozny tribe in tow. That would take too long, and just the sight of his warriors would close the gates of Alba against him for ever. All he needed was a souvenir from the dead prisoner and two bodyguards, Giv and Jamshid. He'd order the rest of the tribe to set up camp beside the No-Man and await his triumphant return. In his absence, command would pass to Kamal, not the brightest of men but cruel enough to keep order.

After careful questioning of those who had captured the Alban, Timur figured out that he had been heading roughly towards the sunset. So to reach Alba, he concluded, the Grozny trio had to journey the opposite way, heading for the point at which the sun first appeared on the horizon. He knew that the settlement was on a mountainside and he had a vague memory of there being hills or mountains of some sort in that region. Once there, he was sure of finding someone he could torture into providing him with more detailed directions.

As it was now dark, Timur went into his tent and lay down. But he was far too excited to sleep. His dream of majesty had been rekindled.

When the Constant slaves responsible for his education had first told him of the legend of the Soterion, he had rejected the idea as superstitious nonsense. Who was interested in the knowledge of the Long Dead, anyway? They had failed. All their building and science had counted for nothing at the time of the Great Death. It hadn't saved them, had it? They had grown soft and feeble, forgotten that what really counted in this world was power, blood and pain. Nothing else mattered.

Information gleaned from Roxanne and other members of her mission had changed Timur's mind. He now appreciated how knowledge might help him in his pursuit of glory. It was within his grasp. All he had to do was hoodwink the Albans and get into the Soterion with a literate Constant to interpret for him, and he would have the knowledge of the Long Dead at his disposal, exclusively. What glorious power that would bring!

There was something else, too. Various of Timur's victims

had mentioned another rumour. As the Long Dead were dying out, it ran, they had been seeking a cure for the Great Death. The details of this so-called Salvation Project, developed but never tested, were said to lie in the Soterion. Now, if he got hold of that, he'd keep it just for himself. So when all others died after eighteen winters, he'd live for fifty, sixty or seventy! Perhaps more – perhaps for ever!

He'd be worshipped and adored. Constants and Zeds from all over the world would prostrate themselves and kiss the feet of Timur the Great, Lord of All Things, Lord of All Men. He'd then be what the Long Dead had called a "god". No, not a god. He would be the God. The Almighty One.

And the key to making this dream come true was that literate and infuriatingly bewitching Constant already making her way towards Alba.

Many thousands of paces away, Roxanne herself was gazing down the long straight road that shimmered and twisted in the merciless late afternoon heat. After crossing the No-Man and turning along Highway 24 in the direction of the rising sun, the mission had tramped across a landscape that became more arid with every day that passed. Tall trees were scarce, replaced by stunted thorns and thick, hostile cactuses. There were no rivers or streams, and Corby's sharp nose had difficulty sniffing out water holes. Day after day, all they knew was dust and heat and sweat.

Signs of the former civilisation were rare. From time to time they came across the crumbling remains of a small settlement, a few sand-strewn homes and a fuel station beside the cracked road. Some had not been looted and in bedrooms long abandoned even by the flies, the bleached bones of former inhabitants lay undisturbed in the stillness.

On the veranda of one remote farmhouse, a worm-eaten rocking chair, whose mummified occupant had fallen asleep long, long ago, swayed aimlessly back and forth in the breeze. On another occasion, as Cyrus and Roxanne were searching a house for shoes, they came across a pair of skull-grinning skeletons lying together on an iron bed. Their yellow, fleshless bones remained entwined as at the moment they died.

Although they were accustomed to death in its many forms, the travellers had never witnessed a scene quite like this. For a while, lightly holding hands, they stared in silence.

"Must have gone at the same time," said Cyrus eventually.

"Fortunate," said Roxanne after another pause. "And beautiful. Like looking in a mirror that sees through time."

Cyrus wondered if this was the moment to mention something that had been on his mind since they first met. "It is several moons since we left Della Tallis, Roxy…"

"No need to go on, Cy." She drew closer to him. "Yes, my time is near – but let's not talk about it."

He held her lovely, sad face between his hands and gently kissed the tear that ran down her cheek. "Don't be sad, Roxy. We are still here, together, and what we are doing will change things, I'm sure. One day," he went on, looking at the bones on the bed, "because of this mission, all Constants will have a chance to live as they lived."

She nodded. "Yes. But there'll still be death at the end of it, won't there? We're not gods."

"You said being morbid wasn't allowed."

"You're right." She glanced down. "I want to give people a chance not to die suddenly and cruelly, as they must have done. That's why we're here, isn't it? Family's the dream that drives me on, Cy. I want men and women to be able to grow old slowly, like they did before the Great Death, to have children, watch over them and guide them."

Her face suddenly brightened. "Do you know, Cleopatra made her son Caesarion joint ruler with her? Mother and son working together, isn't that a beautiful idea?"

"Beautiful, yes."

Roxanne had already told Cyrus about the Third Book of Yonne, a short biography of Cleopatra, the last pharaoh of ancient Egypt. With its talk of gods and goddesses, cruelty and passionate love, campaigns and battles, the story sat uneasily alongside the *IKEA Catalogue* and *Peter Pan*. Not surprisingly, generations of Yonne scholars had struggled to understand the bitter-sweet world of the Long Dead in all its mysterious and changing forms. A queen orders her own sister to be executed, children fight a hook-handed pirate, householders buy kitchens to make their lives easier...

"Such a strange mixture," Roxanne had often said when discussing the Three Books.

Cyrus had suggested the Long Dead remains looked more like the *IKEA* world, not Cleopatra's. And wasn't *Peter Pan* full of kindness and warmth and love? "Seems pretty certain to me," he had concluded, "they managed to make life better. Learned more, lived more. That's what we want back, isn't it?"

The conversation ran through their minds again as they gazed wistfully at the skeleton lovers. When the moment had passed, she took his arm and they went out together into the merciless glare of the desert.

The mission no longer avoided the roads for fear of being spotted. Out here the only other human beings were dead. No Constant settlement could have survived where food and water were so scarce, and not even the Grozny Zeds were able to scavenge a living from this desolate and infertile land.

Food was a problem. They caught and cooked small desert animals – rats, snakes, lizards and the occasional wild dog – and every now and again they came across Long Dead food that was still edible.

The contents of the few cans that had not exploded or leaked were generally putrid. Rats and mice had gnawed their way into most other containers. Once, though, after the mission had been on the road for thirty-five days, Taja had found a large, tightly-sealed glass jar full of rice. Unsure what it was, they nibbled a grain or two and found it pleasant. Roxanne said it looked like the substance she had seen being cooked in a *Catalogue* illustration, so they boiled it in muddy water drawn from an old well.

Roasted lizard spiced with wild herbs and served on a mound of pilau rice was the best meal they had eaten for many days.

The heat forced them to change their pattern of travel. They set out at dawn and walked until the blazing sun drove them into whatever shade they could find. Here they rested till it was cool enough to continue to nightfall. The ceaseless walking took its toll on their bodies. The sun blistered their skin, and when the soles of their shoes wore away they were forced to discard them and continue barefoot.

Sammy suffered most. Life in the Gova settlement had been narrow and regimented, and he was unaccustomed to long periods of physical exercise in the open air. His wooden shoes had dried out and cracked after only a few days. Limping along on bleeding feet, he had no energy to swat away the flies that swarmed over his young face. As a result, his eyes became swollen and red with infection. If they did not find clean water in which to wash regularly, they knew their new friend would soon go blind.

By the time the moon had waxed and waned and begun to wax large again, they scarcely had the energy to speak. When they did, their voices were so harsh and cracked as to be almost unrecognisable. Navid and Cyrus took it in turns to hold Sammy's hand and lead him. Taja brought up the rear, always there, always watching. Ahead, Roxanne drew them onward, ever onward. Heads bowed against the glare, they lurched after her, step after heavy step down that endless, scorching road.

Navid saw it first. Lifting his head to make sure he hadn't fallen behind Roxanne, he found his eyes focusing beyond her, at something in the distance. Dark and shimmering, it could be only one thing. Their destination: the green mountains of Alba. The end was within sight.

The Constant mission was not the only group to have reached its target. The three Grozny travelled light, carrying with them nothing more than a little food and water and a leather bag in the shape of a water melon. Having fortuitously taken a more direct route than their rivals, they avoided the desert, discovered an intact bridge further along the No-Man and arrived safely in the Alba region.

As the Malik had hoped, on two occasions they were helped on their way by unwilling guides. The first was a young Constant breeding slave stolen at night from a small gang of rival Zeds. Timur did not have to work on her for long before she told him what he needed to know: Alba lay midway between the direction of the rising sun and the sun at midday. To express his gratitude for such precise instructions, the Malik killed her rather quicker than he had originally intended.

The second victim, a Constant man, had been the back marker of an Alban patrol returning after three days in the field. Having unwisely left a gap of several paces between himself and the man in front, he was easily knocked down and dragged off without his friends realising what was going on. Fearing an ambush, they did not return to look for him. He proved an obstinate prisoner, however, and it took Timur a while to discover that the Alban stronghold lay only a few thousand paces away on the other side of the valley. He also learned that Roxanne and her accomplices had not yet entered Alba.

Having cheerfully finished off his informant, Timur sat on his own to work out what to do next. After much deliberation, he decided it would be best to approach the Albans and win their confidence before Roxanne and her supporters showed up. That would put him in an excellent position to control whatever happened next. It was time to deliver his message. This he accomplished that same evening, leaving on his own at dusk with the melon-shaped bag and returning shortly before dawn without it.

The mission reached the foothills a day and a half after first sighting them. As the road wound upwards, the climate changed dramatically. Trees reappeared, grass sprang up on the hillsides and nature seized hold of the road, sweeping large sections of it away in avalanches and covering what remained with a blanket of greenery. They found a stream and immediately bathed poor Sammy's puffy eyes and battered, swollen feet.

"That's better!" he gasped between the gulps of cool water proffered by Roxanne. "Soon wash all that muck out my eyes. Then I'll be OK for seeing again, right?"

"With luck," said Roxanne, wiping his face with a piece of cloth. "It's amazing what a good wash can do."

Though her words were optimistic, she was unable to disguise the uncertainty in her voice. The boy was not slow to pick this up.

"Give over, Roxanne! Tell me the truth. I can see you now all that yellow stuff's gone – bit blurry – but I can see you. It'll be fine, yeah?"

Roxanne stood in front of him and placed a hand over his left eye. "Can you still see me, Sammy?"

"Yeah! Of course I can. I've got two eyes, you know!"

Roxanne placed the hand over his right eye. "And now, Sammy? Can you see me now?"

"Not if you covers both of 'em up, Roxanne. Don't be silly!"

She knelt beside him and put an arm round his shoulder. "I wasn't being silly, Sammy. I was covering just your right eye. I'm very, very sorry, Sammy, but your left eye isn't working anymore."

With a tiny cry of anguish, he threw himself onto Roxanne's chest and sobbed inconsolably.

Although they didn't know it at the time, the sight of a boy weeping uncontrollably in the arms of a Zed-marked woman of striking attractiveness probably saved their lives.

Alba's security rested on two things: the position of their settlement on a rocky mountainside, and the skill of their patrols in ensuring no hostile forces approached undetected. Recent events had given this tactic a new importance.

Alban lookouts had the mission under observation from the moment it appeared at the edge of the desert. The person in charge of this operation was Yash, commander of a patrol of six archers. As soon as he was sure of the new arrivals' identity, he sent a young woman running back to the settlement for orders. She returned that afternoon and told him that, however tempted to do so, he was not to speak to anyone in the group under surveillance. Instead, he must immediately kill all of them, except the woman with the Z-shaped tattoo. She alone had to be brought back alive to Alba.

Yash frowned and asked the messenger if she had heard correctly.

"That's exactly what I was told, Yash. The words came straight out of Padmar's mouth."

"Padmar's? Why her? Why not Emir Chima?"

"Well, they told me the Emir had a bad fall while showing the visitor the High Wall," the woman explained nervously. "Not quite certain what happened because I don't think anyone saw it except the visitor, and he was too shocked to say much."

"Go on, Franghad. How's Chima?"

"She's unconscious. Because she can't give orders, Padmar has taken charge. That's why it was she who gave me the orders."

Yash's anxiety was mounting visibly. "And the visitor, was he around?"

"Yes. He was with Padmar – like he nearly always is – and he agreed that her orders were correct."

Yash had never disobeyed the commands of his superiors. Nevertheless, something was not right. The intruders he'd had under observation were as the visitor had said they would be: one male and two female warriors, a Zed woman and a boy. But the visitor also said they would be cruel, and the tattooed woman would be their prisoner. This didn't seem to be the case at all. Judging by their behaviour, the five looked as if they were friends. They chatted together, helped each other over areas where the road had collapsed and took it in turns to guide the boy, who clearly had difficulty seeing.

Watching from the bushes above the glade where the strangers were resting, Yash reckoned the scene below him was as natural as he could imagine. The boy's crying was pitiful, reminding Yash of his own baby son. The Zed woman consoling him, who certainly didn't give the impression of being held against her wishes, looked genuinely upset at the lad's unhappiness. The others, stretched out on the ground with their weapons beside them, looked concerned, too. At least, two of them did. The woman with the dark curly hair seemed more interested in the slimmer of the two male warriors.

I can't do it, Yash said to himself. Whatever my orders, I can't shoot fellow Constants in cold blood. It's only right that I hear what they have to say for themselves. If they're who the visitor says they are, we'll take them back to Alba as prisoners.

Signalling to his men to cover him, he left his hiding place and walked slowly down the slope.

Cyrus saw him first. "Who are you?" he cried, leaping to his feet with his spear at the ready. "A Constant?"

By now Navid and Taja had also taken up their weapons and were standing next to Cyrus in postures of defence.

"Of course," said Yash calmly, keeping his arrow pointing straight at Cyrus' chest. "I'm Yash, a Constant from Alba. And in case you're thinking of fighting, I have five archers in the bushes up there with their bows trained on your hearts. One false move and you will all die."

Cyrus checked the undergrowth where the man had come from. He was right. Five metal arrow heads were visible through the foliage.

"Good," said Yash, who had followed Cyrus' look. "Now it's your turn to answer: who are you?"

Cyrus supposed the man's suspicion was because of Roxanne's tattoo. "Well, Yash, it's not easy to explain, but I'm Cyrus and these are Taja and Navid. We're from Della Tallis, a long way from here. The boy is Sammy, a refugee from the Gova colony."

"And the Zed woman?" demanded Yash, nodding towards Roxanne.

Cyrus smiled. "Ah! That's where it gets complicated."

"I thought so," said Yash. He was already beginning to feel justified in having questioned Padmar's order. "Go on."

"Well, her name is Roxanne. No doubt you'll be pretty pleased to hear she's from Yonne, the only survivor of a mission coming to read the writing on that steel door you've uncovered."

"You mean the Soterion," said Yash calmly.

Cyrus started. "Yes. But how come you're certain that's what it is? You could easily be wrong."

"I'll explain later," replied Yash. He needed to hear what else Cyrus had to say. "Finish your story first, please."

Cyrus was bemused by his insistence. Here they finally were, among the Albans, the people who had requested Yonne help – then why weren't they being welcomed with open arms? And how come this man was so confident of the existence of the Soterion? Roxanne had said the Albans weren't certain what was engraved on the steel door.

"Zeds ambushed the mission Roxanne was on," Cyrus continued. "She was the only survivor."

"And?"

"I think I'd better continue," said Roxanne, carefully setting

186

Sammy aside and standing up. "I was held by the Grozny Zeds for several moons." She pointed to the scar on her forehead. "I was made a slave, tortured – and they gave me this."

"Until, assisted by a companion, you managed to escape," interrupted Yash. The story was as he had heard it from the visitor.

Cyrus stared at Roxanne. Companion? What was this about a companion? He was glad to see her as surprised as himself.

"I escaped on my own," she said icily, her green eyes flashing. "How could I have found a companion in a tribe of Zeds?"

"Not a tall man with unusually pale skin?"

For a second Roxanne looked as if she would strike him. Cyrus took a step towards her, only to be waved away. "No, Cyrus. Thank you. I will deal with this myself." She turned back to Yash. "Would you say that again, please?"

"I'm sorry if I upset you." Taken aback, Yash did as she requested. "All I wanted to know was whether a tall man with an exceptionally white complexion helped you escape?"

The ghastly truth began to dawn on Roxanne. "Why do you ask?"

Yash shrugged. "Simply because he told us that's what he'd done, that's all."

"He told you?" groaned Cyrus. "You spoke to him?" He clenched his fists in angry frustration. "I don't believe it! After all we have been through – "

"Wait a moment." It was Roxanne again, clear and in control. "Let's be absolutely sure, shall we? Tell me, Yash, what is this man's mouth like?"

"His mouth? Well, it's not what we call generous. It's really thin, like a slit. And he doesn't open it very wide, so you don't often see his teeth."

"Thank you. He has a Zed tattoo like mine, yes?"

Yash confirmed this, adding, "Although yours looks more recent than his."

"It is," said Roxanne sharply. "And where is he now, and what does he say his name is?"

"Well, he's back in the settlement. He says his name is Abhay."

Stunned, Cyrus and Roxanne stared at each other in horror and disbelief. They were too shocked to speak, and it was Taja, walking over to Yash in her commanding manner, who took charge.

"Yash," she began, "we have a lot of explaining to do to each other. I'll begin. That man, that visitor you've taken in, is not Abhay. I'm afraid you've all made a terrible error of judgement. His name is Timur, the Malik of the Grozny Zeds. As you surely realise by now, he's the cleverest enemy you'll ever meet."

"And the most despicable," added Roxanne quietly.

Yash's eyes moved searchingly between the two women. "Alright, that's your story. It may sound fairly plausible, but where's the proof?"

"Proof!" gasped Roxanne, close to tears. "I'm the proof, you fool. Isn't it obvious – "

Taja put a hand on her arm. "Gently, Roxanne. Gently. Let me explain." She turned back to Yash. "Right. When you first approached us, you were nervous. Why?"

"I had been ordered to kill you. I wasn't supposed to talk to you."

"Ah! Whose idea was that?"

"Well, it wasn't Padmar's," said Yash slowly. "Yes, I'm sure it must have been the visitor's. Abhay – the man you call Timur."

"I'm sure it was, too." The authority in Taja's voice was almost tangible. "And why do you think he didn't want you to speak to us, Yash?"

"If what you say is right, I suppose it was because he didn't want me to learn the truth."

"Precisely."

The patrol leader was a good man, one strongly tipped by his fellow Albans for a position of high responsibility, and it was only after further discussion that he finally came round to Taja's position. When he did so, he sighed heavily and raised his hands in a gesture of submission.

"To be honest," he confessed, "I sensed there was something wrong with that Zed creature the moment he arrived. I should have followed my gut feeling and turned against him then and there. I feel bad because I didn't – but also because I've now broken my promise always to obey orders. Caught both ways!"

Cyrus laid a hand on his shoulder. "Don't worry, Yash. You're not the first."

"What d'you mean?"

Cyrus explained how, in deciding to become part of the Soterion Mission, both he and Navid and Sammy had faced the same dilemma. Like Yash, in the end they had trusted instinct above upbringing. One of the most important things he had learned over the last few moons, Cyrus added, was that being constant was not always enough.

Yash nodded. "I know what you mean. But it's not easy going against everything you've been taught all your life, is it?"

"Never. Really painful, in fact. But you won't regret it this once, I promise you."

Yash shook his head in an effort to clear his thinking. "Right. I've made my decision. There's no going back now, so let's get on with it. You fill me in with what you know and I'll do the same from my point of view. Then we can work out how to get ourselves out of this terrible mess."

When Yash had summoned the rest of his patrol to join him, Taja and Cyrus outlined what had happened to the mission thus far. When they had finished, Yash told his story.

Slightly less than a moon ago, the severed and mutilated head of Kurav, a member of the third mission to Yonne, had been flung over the walls of Alba in the middle of the night. A crude Z-shape had been carved into the forehead with a knife. The grizzly message confirmed what they feared – like the previous two, Kurav's mission had failed.

Not long afterwards, a tall, Z-marked man with strangely white skin had appeared unarmed and stark naked before the walls of Alba. He came in peace, he said, with wonderful news regarding the Soterion. Might he speak with someone? Padmar leapt at the opportunity. After all, it was she who had suggested employing a Zed – and now, almost by magic, one had appeared. He seemed most personable, too. Almost civilised. She was soon persuaded by his smooth talking and arranged, with Chima's reluctant consent, for him to be allowed into the settlement.

He had been born a Constant, the visitor explained, but was captured by the Zeds in his youth. They had branded him and raised him as one of their own. One day, his tribe had seized and tattooed a literate Constant woman from Yonne. He took pity on her and, after she had explained about the Soterion Mission she had been on, the pair escaped and set out for Alba together. Unfortunately, they fell in with some very devious Constants from Della Tallis who forced the woman to join them. These traitors planned to use her to steal the secrets of the Soterion for themselves and thereby gain dominance over all other Constants.

"And the Albans believed these lies?" exclaimed Cyrus, scarcely able to credit what he was hearing.

"There were some early doubts, of course," said Yash. "But they didn't last long. Now the majority of the people almost worship him, hailing him as a sort of saviour. Whatever he says, goes. Not many shared my worries; or if they did they kept it to themselves. Most Albans are so keen to get behind that steel door, they'll follow anyone who promises to help them do it.

"The job of my patrol was to watch out for your arrival, kill everyone except the tattooed woman, and take her to Abhay –"

"Timur," corrected Roxanne.

"Sorry, Timur. Once he had her with him, he said he'd open the Soterion and share its secrets with everyone!"

"Fat chance!" grunted Navid.

"Worse still," concluded Yash miserably, "it now looks as if he's got rid of our Emir, Chima. That leaves Padmar and her friend Timur in charge of the whole settlement. I tell you, Cyrus, we're going to have our hands full sorting out this shambles."

"Exactly," said Cyrus. "We'll do everything we can to help, of course, but you know the lie of the land, Yash. So, what's the plan?"

10
Into Alba

Yash brushed away the strand of red hair that had fallen across his face. "Plan, Cyrus?" he shrugged. "Wish I could think of one!"

"What if we all just march back to Alba and say who we are," suggested Navid in what turned out to be the longest sentence he had ever spoken, "and tell 'em that the bloke who says his name is Abhay is really Timur, chief of the Grozny, and then they'll arrest him, or whatever, and we can get on with opening this Soterion?"

"Yes, that's the obvious thing to do," said Yash, "but it's too risky."

Navid frowned. "I don't get it, Yash. How's it risky?"

"It's like Yash said," explained one of the other Alban archers, a tall, thin woman whose black hair reached to the leather belt at her waist. "Timur has kind of planned for that. He's told everyone that you lot, the Constants from Della Tallis, are clever and tricky. If you now turn up and call him a liar, he'll say that's precisely what he'd warned us against: you've got Roxanne and have turned her against Padmar and himself."

"What's more," chipped in another of Yash's patrol, "we've disobeyed orders in not killing you. In Alban eyes that makes us not the sort of people you'd trust. Traitors almost. You're a Constant – you know what disobeying orders means, don't you?"

Cyrus nodded. Yes, he knew alright. He remembered vividly how torn he had been between obeying Emir Leiss and following the alluring Z-marked refugee with her extraordinary story of a Soterion. He glanced across at Roxanne to find her looking at him. She had read his mind and was smiling.

Poor, lovely Roxy! he thought. She looks desperately tired. Not surprising considering what she's been through, leading us, driving us day after day across that blazing wilderness. It was her spirit, her will, her strength that kept us going. Understandably it had taken a lot out of her, he now realised. She hadn't looked so exhausted since the day of her escape from the Grozny.

Taja's voice brought him back to the present. "And if you return empty-handed and say you've never seen us, wouldn't they believe that, either?"

Yash shook his head. "I've reported seeing you."

"But couldn't you say it was a mistake, that you'd got the wrong people?"

Taja was more animated than she had been for a long time, Cyrus thought. Also more positive. Had she finally accepted that Roxanne had been telling the truth all along? And if so, what had made her change her mind?

"No, it was clear I'd seen you," said Yash, shaking his head. "All the details were right. And we've been out on patrol much longer than usual. If we go back empty-handed now, we'll be under all kinds of suspicion."

"And if you don't go back at all?" asked Cyrus.

"No good either," replied the woman with the long black hair. "Even if you're a day late, they send out people to bring you in. A while back, when an entire patrol never came home, every able-bodied person in Alba was sent to look for them. Too late, as it turned out. The Zeds had got them. Murdering swine!"

"You mean," said Cyrus, "that if you don't show up soon, we'll have goodness knows how many Defenders –"

"About three hundred."

"Three hundred! Three hundred Defenders swarming all over this mountainside looking for you?"

"Probably," confirmed Yash with a smile of grim resignation. "And they'd put a massive guard on the Soterion, too, in case you had somehow avoided or killed us and were trying to get in there unnoticed."

For a few moments, they stood around without saying a word, confounded by the impossibility of their position. Cyrus became aware of the stream babbling and splashing behind him. It's mocking us, he thought, laughing at our puny human worries. What does it care? It'll go on chattering to itself long after we're gone. He took a deep breath. For Roxanne's sake, for the sake of all they had been through, for the dead Zavar, for poor, half-blind Sammy, for the honour of all of them, there was only one option.

"If you agree, Yash," he said, advancing into the middle of the clearing, "this is what we'll do –"

No one ever discovered what Cyrus had in mind. Before he could say anything further, Taja interrupted him. It was the old Taja, the strong, sharp and forceful Mudir of the West Tower. "I'm sure your plan's a good one, Cyrus. Even so, I think you'll find mine's better."

Before he could interrupt, she went on, "There's only one certain way out of this: Yash and his archers must return to Alba with Roxanne."

Gasps of astonishment greeted the suggestion. "You can't be serious!" spluttered Cyrus, dismissing Taja's recent agreeableness as a front.

"Listen, Cyrus, will you?" she snapped. "It's the best option by far. We'll go back to Alba while you and Roxanne try to get into the Soterion. Navid can protect Sammy and stand guard."

"Er, sorry, but I don't get it, Taja," said Navid, running his fingers through his hair. "To begin with, who's this 'we' going back to Alba?"

She gave him a quick smile. "The patrol and myself."

"But you said Roxanne…"

"Exactly, Navid. Mark me with the sign of a Zed and who'll know the difference? I'll go as Roxanne. While I'm confusing Timur and Padmar, Cyrus and the real Roxanne will have a chance of getting into the Soterion. If Timur can get away with pretending to be someone else, why can't I?"

Roxanne came forward, palm outstretched. Taja took it without a word and, for the first time, the two women embraced.

"Thank you, Taja," said Roxanne solemnly. "This is the bravest thing anyone could offer to do. Yet I'm afraid it won't work. Timur will immediately see you're not me and then he'll…Well, quite frankly, it terrifies me to think what he'll do. You can't imagine how evil he is, Taja. He's all deviousness, all cruelty."

"I'm prepared to risk it," said Taja, standing back and looking Roxanne straight in the face. "Anyway, if – or when – Timur does recognise me, what can he do?"

She turned towards the archer patrol. "Yash will tell him that he has killed all the unmarked Constants, as he was ordered, and brought back the woman with the Zed tattoo. Then I'll confess that I'm not Roxanne but Taja."

No one said a word.

"I'll explain to him," Taja went on, "that because we were worried the Albans wouldn't trust someone with a Zed tattoo, Roxanne hid her mark with mud while I drew a Zed mark on myself with charcoal. I did this, I'll explain, for Roxanne's sake, to see how the Albans would react to someone looking as if they were a Zed. How ironic, I'll tell them as I weep for the deaths of my friends, that a false tattoo saved my life while Roxanne died because she had covered up her real one!

"It's the perfect way to outwit Timur: the evil genius foiled by the cleverness of his own plan!"

It was a brilliant idea, Cyrus agreed, though terribly dangerous. And he still didn't know why Taja was suddenly willing not only to accept Roxanne's story of the Soterion, but to risk her life for it.

"Taja," he said slowly, "you're right – your idea probably is the best way to divert Timur while we try to get into the Soterion. However, as Roxy says, you're putting yourself in real danger. If Timur finds out what's actually going on, well…"

He left the sentence unfinished, partly because he didn't want to spell out what might happen and partly because, after a few seconds, Taja completed it for him.

"…he'll kill me, no doubt – if Padmar lets him – in the vilest way imaginable. I'm ready. I don't have much time remaining anyway, so I might as well do something useful."

Navid's brow furrowed. "Is that really why you came on the mission, Taja?" he asked. "You joined us to help, not to check up on Roxanne?"

Taja shrugged. "Look, Navid, as you know, I'm not a sentimental person and every moment we waste talking will make our task more difficult…But I'll say only this – and it's my last word on the subject, OK?"

Navid nodded.

"You're right to be confused," she went on, "because I was myself, for a long time. I didn't trust Roxanne. I'm not sure why. Maybe I didn't believe anyone would give up everything and go through hell for a dream. I wouldn't have done it myself."

She gave her former rival a strange look, admiration blending awkwardly with envy. "But I've watched her, seen her determination, heard her story and had it confirmed by the behaviour of Timur and the words of Yash and his patrol.

"And now I see I was wrong: there are people who act for the good of others. They think beyond themselves, of the community and of the future. I suppose those who set up the Soterion were like that. So before it's too late, I want – for once in my life – to make a difference."

"Anyway," she added, suddenly changing her tone, walking over to Cyrus and putting her arms round his neck, "I came along because I wanted to be with this man, wherever he went."

Cyrus smiled awkwardly and shook his head.

"No need for anyone to pretend now, Cyrus," she laughed. "Why do you think I've been watching you so carefully, eh? I was hoping when you had learned to read and Roxanne was out of the way, we could finish this mission together. You and me, saviours of the Constants!

"Foolish and unkind, I know – but understand how I feel about you, Cyrus. And always have. Always will."

Taja, the unsentimental, iron-willed Taja, raised a hand to her face to hide the trembling of her bottom lip. The moment passed as swiftly as it had arisen. Regaining her composure, she turned to Yash and told him to escort her to Alba without further delay. "No tears, no goodbyes," she insisted. "Not a word, please. Let's just go."

As the evening closed in, the two groups made their hasty preparations. The tall Alban woman helped Taja straighten her hair by dampening it with water, and etched the mark of a Zed on her forehead with charcoal. As the patrol would arrive in the dark, she said, there was a fair chance that Timur would not learn of the deception until morning. Taja, after a few quick words with Roxanne, tried to imagine how she should react on meeting a man who had once raped and tortured her. It wasn't easy.

Meanwhile, Yash explained to Cyrus precisely where the Soterion was and how best to get there without encountering an Alban patrol. The mysterious iron door lay in a cave set into a steep, wooded slope on the opposite side of the mountain from Alba. The entrance had been partly blocked by a rockfall, then further obscured by a screen of trees and bushes that had grown up since the Great Death.

Following its discovery, the mouth to the cave had been cleared, although it was still difficult to find unless one knew precisely where to look. Even if someone did stumble across it, they would find the entrance blocked by a locked steel door. As a consequence, the Albans left the place comparatively lightly guarded. Yash said two warriors kept a permanent lookout above the site and two more at the entrance to the cave itself. The principal problem would be the upper guards. Both carried horns and had orders to blow them at the slightest hint of danger. The noise would alert the guards below and, if the wind was in the right direction, carry as far as the walls of Alba.

And another thing, added Yash, he hoped Cyrus and Roxanne would be able to reach the door without causing the guards unnecessary injury. All four were his friends, especially Asal and Shyad, the horn carriers on the upper station.

When all was ready, as a gibbous moon rose over the distant desert, Taja and her escort walked briskly out of the clearing and took the ruined road for Alba. As he watched the indomitable Mudir of the West Tower disappear from view without a word of farewell or a backward glance, Cyrus felt a wave of sadness sweep through him. Experience and instinct conspired to whisper that Zavar would not be the only one of the party to die before the mission was accomplished.

Cyrus became aware of Roxanne standing beside him. "Do you think she'll be alright, Roxy?" he asked quietly, pushing back the hair from her forehead and kissing the puckered scar.

"I don't know, Cy. I hope so. She's an incredibly brave woman."

"And a sad one, too, though she did her best to hide it." He paused for a moment. "I wonder what made her finally change her mind about you?"

Roxanne lifted her tired face towards him. "A woman's instinct, I suppose."

"Not a very sharp one. It took her ages to see what most people knew from the moment you came over the barricade: that you're honest and true, and this thing on your forehead is a lie."

"Do you blame her, Cy?" Standing on her toes, she slipped her arms round his neck and pressed herself close against him. "Whether you do or not, her instinct picked up something else much more quickly. I think it was that which changed her mind."

Deep within him, Cyrus felt the first ripple of panic. No! Please, not now!

Seeing the look in his eyes, she held him tighter still. "Look at me Cy! Look at me!"

Gently, slowly, she removed her arms from round his neck

and turned her face to the moonlight. "You see, Cyrus? I believe Taja noticed it. That's why she kept saying we had to hurry."

Cyrus had seen it before, many, many times. Back in Della Tallis, it was an everyday occurrence. Sad, indeed, yet unavoidable. One just accepted it. But not Roxy, not the loveliest human being he had ever met...

Words stuck in his throat. "How long?" he said eventually, staring in disbelief at the face that was the same and yet subtly, cruelly different.

"Maybe five days? I first felt it when we were in the desert. I didn't want to tell anyone in case it made them less determined to carry on. The dust in my hair helped – covered the strands that were going grey. I checked when we got here and saw my reflection in the stream."

"Oh, Roxy! And all I said was that you looked tired! How could I have been so blind?" He turned her round and clasped her to him. "I don't want you to go!"

"Silly man!" she smiled, refusing to be drawn into morbidity. "I won't! At least, not yet. Listen, I've been working it out – here's what I reckon.

"During my Death Month I'm growing older – in Long Dead terms – by about two winters each day. Now, according to the Third Book, a man named Caesarion lived to the age of seventy-five. That's like a Death Month of twenty-eight days. Five or six of mine have gone; therefore, if I'm like him, I've got twenty days or more of life! That's enough time for us, isn't it, Cy?"

Cyrus had no words to reply. Through the pain of his wretchedness, he found but one consolation. It did not have to be like this. Somewhere, beyond the black mountain that loomed over them, lay a cave, and in that cave lay hope, the hope that had inspired Roxanne and that now made him determined to fulfil this mission, though every Zed in the world barred his path. Nothing would stop him. It would be his memorial, his everlasting tribute to the woman he loved.

For much of the night, the four Constants followed the route given to them by Yash. It wound up and up, passing through tangled woods and across rocky slopes till it levelled out on a small plateau overlooking distant hills. Before them, scarcely ten paces away, the Tallins saw a pair of shadowy figures. Good, thought Cyrus, only two. That means Taja's plan has worked and Timur is unaware what's going on. Now for the guards.

Cyrus and Navid had spent some time working out how best to neutralise the upper lookouts. The safest tactic, Navid had suggested, was simply to sneak up on them and cut their throats. Bearing in mind Yash's request, Cyrus overruled him. The men were Constants, he said, not Zeds. Violence should be a last resort.

Leaving Roxanne and Sammy in the shadow of the trees, the Defenders spread out left and right on either side of the lookouts. Then, drawing on years of experience, they crept as close as possible without being seen.

"Hey, Asal!" hissed Cyrus from behind a boulder, hoping that the silhouette nearest to him really was that of a woman. "It's Yash!"

The figure instinctively reached for her horn.

"No! Whatever you do, don't blow that thing!"

The second figure came up to see what was happening. "What's going on, Asal?" he muttered. "Want me to blow?"

"It's Yash," said Asal uncertainly, peering into the darkness. "Or someone saying he is."

"Can't be," grunted Shyad, lifting his horn. "Yash's lot are patrolling the slopes overlooking the desert. They're watching for that lot Abhay said were coming."

"Yes, I was there," said Cyrus in a loud whisper, rising up enough for part of him to be visible. "I've found the Constants. That's why I've come to talk to you. I've got some news – really important – and you're the only ones I can trust. Asal...Shyad... Please!"

The two guards looked at each other and shrugged. "Alright, Yash," said Asal cautiously, raising her sword. "Come out so we can see you. And no funny business, OK? One hint of anything tricky and Shyad will blow, got it?"

Cyrus stood up and moved a few steps closer.

"Closer!" called Shyad, lowering his horn. "I want to see your face. You don't sound like – "

"It's not!" cried Asal. "Quick! Blow that horn, Shy!"

The warning came too late. As Shyad went to lift the instrument to his lips, it was dashed from his hand and fell with a clatter to the ground. He spun round to confront his assailant.

Navid had crept up behind the lookouts as they were concentrating on Cyrus and now stood, axe raised, half a pace from their unprotected chests. "If you as much as flinch," he commanded quietly, "I'll cut you in half. Throw down

204

your weapons!"

The rest of the operation fell into place as Cyrus had hoped. It did not take long to explain to Asal and Shyad what was going on. When they heard that Yash, a good and trusted friend, had joined with the Tallins, they had no hesitation in following suit. Like the patrol leader, they admitted that they had had their doubts about Abhay and had accepted him only out of loyalty to the Emir and Padmar. After sharing their rations with their new friends, who had not eaten properly since that morning, they led them down the slope towards the entrance of the cave.

"This is it, Roxy!" whispered Cyrus, taking her hand. "We've made it!"

It certainly seemed so. Although one of the lower guards refused to go along with the "conspirators" as he called them and had to be bound and gagged, the other willingly joined the growing band of rebels.

The first streaks of dawn glimmered through the canopy of leaves as Cyrus and Roxanne, side by side, walked slowly into the dark opening. It was smaller than they had anticipated, perhaps only two-and-a-half paces square. A few steps in, they found their way blocked by a massive, moss-encrusted wall of rusty steel into which, on the left, a small door had been set.

Roxanne's hands trembled with excitement as she knelt in front of the door. "Look what it says, Cyrus," she whispered her voice breaking with sobs. "The Soterion! I don't believe it! We've done it! We've done it!"

Cyrus knelt and put his arm round her. He couldn't help noticing that she already felt different. She was more angular and her bones were nearer the surface. "You brilliant, wonderful woman!" he said. "Come on! Let's get inside!"

"THE SOTERION," Roxanne read, running her fingers over the rust-encrusted steel to make sure she understood the letters correctly. "CONSTRUCTED IN HOPE FOR THE FUTURE OF ALL HUMANITY. 2019."

She stopped. "That's all there is, Cy. It doesn't tell us how to get in. There's no keyhole, either." She straightened up and leaned back against the rocky wall. "We can't get this far and not be able to get in, can we? That'd be too cruel, Cy. Too cruel."

"Of course not, Roxy! Move over a bit and let me have a look." Cyrus knelt before the door. True, there was no keyhole, just writing and a raised depiction of a book welded onto the steel. He looked at the image more carefully. No, it wasn't welded on, it was held by a single rivet at the top. One rivet meant it should swing. However, when he tried to push the plate to one side, he found it had corroded onto the wall.

He picked up a stone from the floor of the cave and tapped the edge of the cover. Slowly, bit by bit, it swung aside to reveal a patch of clean bright steel. In its centre, clear and unobstructed, was a keyhole. Beneath it, etched in tiny writing, was a message.

"You're the reader, Roxy – better than me, anyway. What's it say?"

She stooped down beside him again and read:

THE KEY TO HOPE OF ALL MANKIND

BENEATH THE LION YOU WILL FIND

"Mmm, they're not making it easy for us, are they?" Cyrus muttered.

He stood up and turned away from the door, calling quietly, "Hey Asal! Shyad! Here, quick!"

The two Albans hurried into the cave. "Yes?" said Shyad, staring at the door. "What've you found?"

"Where's the lion?"

"Lion? What's a lion got to do with it? I thought you were looking for those book things?"

"I am. They're behind this door. But the key's underneath some lion."

"There aren't any lions around here," chipped in Asal, "unless you mean that stone one – we call it the 'statue' – near the well."

"That's got to be it," cried Cyrus. "And that's where we're going next!"

Roxanne laid a hand on Cyrus' arm. "Don't rush, Cy," she said calmly. "I've got days left, so let's make sure we don't fail at the last."

Cyrus looked at her. She was right, of course, as always. They had no idea what was going on inside the walls of Alba. Clearly Taja's deception had bought them precious time. But it was now full daylight – surely Timur knew by now he had been tricked? Perhaps he was also suspicious of Yash's story about killing the true Roxanne along with the other members of the mission?

Cyrus summoned Navid, Sammy and the third guard, Melker, to join them. After explaining the riddle of the lion, he asked the Albans the best way of getting hold of the key.

Shyad told him the image of a lion, carved from stone during the time of the Long Dead, rested on a plinth beside the well at the centre of the Alba community. It was impossible to reach without being seen. The solid statue was eight hands tall, added Melker. It would take at least three people to move it and get at anything underneath – assuming the key really was there.

"What about you?" said Cyrus. "Could you go back and move the statue for us?"

Shyad shook his head. "Tricky. There are always a few archers in the square, guarding the well. And like Melker said, what'd happen if we managed to shove over the statue and then didn't find the key? We'd be strung up for vandalism!"

"He's right," added Asal. "It can't be done secretly, Cyrus. We need time as well as security."

"OK, let's try a different approach," said Roxanne, who had been listening carefully to their conversation. "Tell me, does everyone really support Timur, the man you call Abhay?"

"Just about everyone," said Melker.

Asal disagreed. Hadn't all three of them changed sides quickly enough when told the truth? So had Yash and his patrol. The relief guards would be coming soon, and there was a good chance they could be persuaded to join the rebellion. That would give them four members of the mission, Yash's six archers, Taja, and seven Alban guards – nineteen in all.

"Tough fight," observed Navid gloomily. "Nineteen against three hundred. Wouldn't like to be one of the nineteen."

"I don't think it's a matter of fighting," answered Roxanne. "It's more to do with persuading. What do you think, Asal?"

"Well, I reckon if a large enough group of us go back in peace and tell them what we know, and they see you, Roxanne – well,

I think quite a lot would come over. At least, they wouldn't fight against us. What do you think, Shy?"

Shyad shrugged. "Maybe."

"Melker?"

"Risky, but it might work."

"The longer we wait," said Cyrus, "the greater the chance that Timur will find out what's going on. And once he does, I imagine Taja, Yash and all his patrol will be finished – and we won't have a chance, either. Let's wait until the relief guards show up, get them to join us, and then all go into Alba together. Agreed?"

With a mixture of grunts and raised fists, they all accepted Cyrus' proposal. Shortly afterwards, as they had planned, their numbers were swollen by the four relief guards. They were also helped by the surprise conversion of the man they had been forced to tie up. Having overheard their discussions, he said, he would now throw in his lot with his friends. That brought their number to twelve: eight Albans, two Tallins, Roxanne the Yonner and little Sammy. From a military point of view, they were puny. But armed with the truth, they hoped their strength was greater than mere numbers.

The rebel party reached the high stone walls of Alba in good time. However, as they approached, shouting cheerfully to the guards, they were dismayed to find the gates hurriedly closing against them.

"Hey!" called Shyad, looking up at the Defenders on the platform on the top of the wall. "You know who we are.

Open up!"

"Sorry, Shyad," came the reply. "Not our decision. Padmar says no one's to be allowed in without her personal permission. Not even you lot. And who are those other people with you?"

Beckoning Navid, Roxanne and Sammy to his side, Cyrus came forward.

"Friends!" he began. "We are Constants and we come in peace. I am Cyrus and this is my friend Navid; we're Defenders from the community of Della Tallis. The lad is from the Gova settlement and we are here to escort and protect this woman, Roxanne from Yonne.

"Please don't be put off by her tattoo. She's the only survivor from the first mission. She's from Yonne and can read. She's here to help you by opening the Soterion. Time is short because she is in her Death Month. You must let us in."

The announcement took the guards by surprise. For some time they argued among themselves before one of them called down, "We don't believe you! Roxanne's already here!"

Cyrus was on the point of replying when two more figures appeared on the platform. One was a small, dark woman in a purple cloak with a hood over most of her short-cropped hair. The other Cyrus recognised at once, although he had never previously set eyes on him. Tall, deathly pale, with long, silver-white hair that only partially hid the vivid scar on his forehead, he could only be one man. Timur.

Roxanne gasped. Although several moons had passed since she had last seen him, he still terrified her. Instinctively feeling her distress, Cyrus, Sammy and Navid closed in around her.

As they did so, Timur began to laugh. It was a high, thin, nasty sound, like tearing tin. Although fearful, Cyrus sensed it went on too long to be natural. It was a cover. The dreadful Malik was playing for time, trying to come to terms with what was going on. As Cyrus suspected, he had seen through Taja's disguise, but until this moment he had not realised that Yash had deceived him, too.

Roxanne was not dead. She was not in his service, either. And never would be. It was too horribly clear: the woman from Yonne had beaten him. She would unlock the Soterion, she would share its secrets, she would be honoured. And he, Timur the Terrible, would be excluded, condemned to spend the rest of his life a mere Malik of miserable Zeds. He would never be all-powerful…He would never be God!

For the first time in his life, the leader of the Grozny was lost for words. But as the cornered rat bites deepest, so at this moment he was at his most deadly. If power and glory were not to be his, then they would be no one's.

In his right hand Timur held what Cyrus had taken to be a staff. Now, too late, he saw that it was in fact a javelin. With a scream of rage, the monstrous Zed raised the weapon high above his shoulder and, all in the same movement, hurled it with tremendous force straight at Roxanne.

11
The Soterion

While the other members of the mission were pursuing the path towards tragedy at the gates of Alba, Taja was holding an ill-fated course of her own. Through the gathering gloom, she followed Yash and his patrol in silence, preoccupied with her own thoughts. However, when the track widened so it was no longer necessary to walk in single file, Jannat, the tall, long-haired archer, drew alongside her and tried to strike up a conversation.

At first the exchange was one-sided, the Tallin responding to Jannat's questions with a blunt "yes" or "no". Gradually, though, she began to open up. The grim look on her face eased, and by the time they reached their destination she was talking more freely than she had done for many years.

The two women began by comparing the customs and lifestyles of Alba and Della Tallis. In many ways they were similar. Both were illiterate communities, although they knew of books and writing. They shared the Constant values of courage, respect, unity and duty, and held men and women in equal honour. Leaders were chosen by handshows, the Alban equivalent for "Mudir" being "Konnel".

Jannat, who was hoping to be a Konnel after the next winter, guessed correctly that Taja was already a Mudir.

Taja gave her a quizzical look. "Is it obvious?"

Jannat laughed. "We say that leaders are born, not made. I only have to look at you to see you're a born leader. It's obvious."

The subject led to one of the principal differences between the two communities. Whereas Della Tallis was essentially agricultural, Alba was a military settlement. The tradition went back as long as anyone could remember – legend said Long Dead soldiers had helped build its high walls of stone and concrete, the terraces rising up the lower slopes of the mountain, and the dwellings clustered around a broad square. The carved stone lion that stood beside the well in the centre of the square was believed to be another gift from these military forefathers.

Taja learned, somewhat to her surprise, that in Alba weapons training began at the age of eight. All Defenders paraded once a month in the main square. Discipline was stricter than in Della Tallis, too, with public floggings for those who stepped out of line. To keep up the strength of the defence force, as far as possible reproduction was regulated. Between the ages of thirteen and fifteen, all women were expected to have at least one child before returning to military and agricultural duties. Their offspring were raised communally by a team of younger women supervised by four Konnels. Relations between men and women over the age of fifteen were not expected to result in the birth of further children.

Jannat talked for a moment about her child, Parmin, then asked Taja whether she had any children. No, came the curt response, she had not. They walked on for a few steps. "I don't like to talk about it, Jannat," she added in a softer tone. "You understand, don't you?"

"Of course."

"Children mean you are never forgotten – and I don't want to be forgotten. I don't want to live and die and disappear like an insect. If I had children, they would talk about their mother, and their children would talk about their grandmother, and so on. But that won't happen to me."

"It's the same for nearly everyone," replied Jannat. "I don't suppose Parmin will ever remember me when I'm gone – and his children certainly won't!"

"But that's what I don't want!" retorted Taja, suddenly animated. "I'm intelligent and able! My spirit should not flare and burn out, leaving ashes to blow away in the wind. That's why I hoped Cyrus and I could find the Soterion together and give its secrets to the world."

The archer laid a hand on Taja's arm, only to have it brushed aside. "I don't need sympathy, Jannat! Nor do I deserve it. Listen, on the way here I did something dishonourable. One of the men in our band was injured – I hastened his death so he would not slow us up. I sacrificed him. Now I have a chance of redemption, even sacrificing myself if necessary… "

"I promise you," said Jannat, aware now that Taja, despite her hard shell, was as vulnerable as every other Constant, "that you will be long remembered. Whatever happens when we get to Alba, you will always be the person who risked everything for others."

"Is that really what I'm doing?" muttered Taja. "Behaving like Roxanne?"

"Yes, it is. You didn't have to leave Cyrus and the others and come with us, did you?"

"No, I suppose that's true. I didn't." Taja's voice became lower, as if she had to force the words from her throat. "Well, Jannat, if things go wrong – you know, if I don't survive to see the end of this mission – please tell Cyrus what you just told me."

"That you are risking all you had for a principle, like Roxanne?"

"Yes."

Jannat smiled. "Don't worry, Taja. I think he knows that already."

It was the middle of the night by the time Yash's band reached the small patrol door in the settlement wall. Following the usual procedure, they identified themselves with a password before the bars across the door were pulled back and they were allowed in.

Unused to Alban formality, Taja was surprised by the way the patrol reported back. The archers, standing on either side of her in a row, had their weapons checked to ensure they were undamaged. Yash then informed the Duty Konnel what had happened, pointing to Taja and calling her Roxanne, as planned.

The Konnel peered at Taja's tattoo in the moonlight, nodded and ordered her to be held in the guardroom until Abhay verified her identity in the morning. The officer did not want to be responsible for a Z-marked woman wandering freely around the settlement in the dark.

When Yash asked the Konnel why he did not report to Abhay and Padmar immediately, the man hesitated for a moment before repeating what he had been told. The acting Emir, he explained with obvious embarrassment, had given orders not to be disturbed. She and Abhay had important matters to discuss and wished to be left alone.

Discuss important matters all night? thought Taja. Padmar had obviously fallen for more than Timur's promise of unlocking the secrets of the Soterion. Was there no limit to this monster's dreadful powers? Not long afterwards, her mind still swirling with curiosity and fear of what lay ahead, she lay down on a rough bench in the guardroom and fell into an uneasy sleep.

Early the following morning, Yash led his archers into the parade square and stood next to the lion to wait for Padmar. Looking tired and flushed, she appeared with Timur at her side and began questioning the patrol about its mission. Her partner, his tattoo covered by a huge black hat, loomed over the diminutive Konnel like an evil puppet-master.

"Excuse me, acting Emir of the Alba," he interrupted with oily good manners. "May I put a question or two to our friend Yash?"

Padmar's eyes were drained of all judgement as she gazed up at him. "Of course, Abhay!"

"Thank you, Padmar. Now, Yash, tell me this instant – no, please forgive my rudeness – I mean, do fill me in on the success of your exemplary patrol. You rescued Roxanne, for instance, my old Constant friend?"

"We did."

Timur's eyes flashed with delight. "And where is she?"

"In the guardroom, as the Duty Konnel ordered."

Timur rubbed his hands together, struggling to keep himself under control. This was too good to be true! These batbrained Albans had delivered Roxanne to him without realising what they were doing. With a little not-so-gentle persuasion, she would be only too eager to put the secrets of the Soterion into his grateful hands!

"And you are sure it is she?" he continued eagerly. "You've seen the tattoo – the foul mark of a Zed – cruelly burned on her, like mine?"

"She's branded, yes," Yash replied cautiously. He hated lying, though he had no choice.

Timur's eyes narrowed slightly. This fool wasn't trying to hide something from him, was he? "And you killed her escort of Constants – all of them?"

"Shot dead with arrows and buried, yes."

"I expect that pleased Roxanne, didn't it?" asked Timur, his whole body writhing with anticipation at how Yash would respond to his wickedly barbed question.

Yash hesitated, fatally. What was he supposed to reply? Timur had said Roxanne was a friend whom Cyrus held against her wishes. But Yash now knew what Timur had known all

218

along – that this was a lie. He played for time.

"Pleased her, Abhay?"

The Great Zed could contain himself no longer. "Toadpizzle!" he screamed. "You know what I mean! What did she say when you told her she was coming back to me, the Mali – " He stopped just in time, biting his tongue in the process.

"She doesn't want to meet you again, Abhay," said Yash, staring in disgust at the trickle of blood running down the ice-white face.

The besotted Padmar started. "Oh Abhay! You said –"

Timur cut her short. "She lies! Poisonous, worm-ridden lies!" he cried. "Of course she's thrilled at the prospect of being reunited with me. Am I the only one who tells the truth?"

Yash resisted the temptation to give the obvious answer.

"I will see for myself," Timur continued. Swinging round, he ran off with enormous strides in the direction of the guardroom. For a moment, Yash thought of following him to protect Taja from possible harm. Having witnessed a side of Timur not seen before, he feared greatly for her safety. But he stayed where he was – revealing the truth now might jeopardise their whole plan.

Padmar, mesmerised by Timur's false charms, watched until he was out of sight then turned back to Yash. "On that man," she said, "hangs the fate of our whole community. Yash, I hope you haven't been disloyal to Alba."

"No, I have not, Konnel Padmar," he replied firmly, refusing to link her with the position of Emir. "We brought back a Z-marked woman, as Abhay asked."

She looked up at him, a quizzical expression on her small, round face. "Well, Abhay will soon be back with his friend and we will know the truth. In the meantime, fill me in on the details of your patrol."

Timur was gone longer than expected. By the time he reappeared, walking alone up the stony slope from the guardroom, Yash and his archers had related their full story. They made a good job of it, moving on from the truth to weave an elaborate fabrication of slaying the Constants and capturing the woman with the Zed tattoo.

"Well, Abhay?" asked Padmar as he approached. Ignoring her, he stormed straight up to Yash and punched him viciously in the face. "Ignorant snakescum!" he screeched. As the archer reeled backwards, Timur raised his fist to strike again.

"No!" cried Padmar, grabbing his arm. "That is not our way, Abhay! Tell me first! Please!"

Trembling with rage, the Malik of the Grozny gave Padmar a look of indescribable scorn. "Not your way?" he mimicked, his high-pitched voice resembling hers with unkind accuracy. "What is your way? To lie and cheat like your frogspawn warriors who bring in the wrong woman, eh? Don't you understand? The woman this incompetent insect has brought in is not Roxanne!"

Yash wiped the blood from his mouth. If he had needed any proof of Roxanne's description of Timur as "all evil", he had it now. This Z-marked thing was indeed a beast, a fiendishly clever one. Padmar might have fallen deeper into his trap than others, seduced into overlooking his obvious wickedness, but at first hadn't they all been tempted there by his brilliant deception?

Now look where it had got them! Yash decided to speak out before the devilish intruder dug his claws in any deeper.

He had barely opened his mouth, when they were interrupted by three men running into the square. "Konnel Padmar! Konnel Padmar!" cried one of them. "You are needed at the gate right now!"

"What is it?"

"A force of about a dozen warriors, including all the Soterion guards, is headed this way. There's a child with them, and a woman with what looks like a Zed tattoo! The gate guards don't know whether to let them in or not."

Padmar glanced at Timur. His demeanour had switched yet again, and for the first time she felt a flicker of mistrust. The quivering fury of a few seconds ago had melted into eager anticipation as he took in what the messenger had said. A woman with a tattoo? Was it possible?

"Shall we go, dear Padmar?" he enquired with exaggerated civility. "This might be interesting."

The need for decisive action forced Padmar temporarily to ignore the shadow lurking at the back of her mind. She may have lost her judgement on one issue, but for everyday matters she retained the leadership and decision-making skills that had made her a Konnel. "We will go to the gate at once," she ordered. "Run ahead and tell them to do nothing till I get there."

Ordering Yash and his archers not to move a step in her absence, she hurried off towards the gate. The black-hatted Timur, stalking her like the raven of death, followed closely behind.

Once the Konnel was out of the square, Jannat came across to Yash. "Now we know for sure, what are we going to do?"

"After coming this far," said Yash, speaking with difficulty because of the cut on his lip, "there's no going back."

Jannat nodded. "We're all agreed on that, Yash. His behaviour was vile, wasn't it? But I think there might be worse."

"What do you mean?"

"Did you see what was on his shirt?"

"Yes, my blood!"

"No," frowned Jannat. "It was there when he came back from the guard room. I'm afraid it might be someone else's."

Padmar and Timur were nearing the wall as Cyrus finished speaking. His words had carried clearly to them, confusing the Konnel and sending her partner into a fit of violent quivering. Calling up to the guards to remember their orders, the pair clambered swiftly up the ladder to join them. Timur knocked his hat off on the way up and, such was his urgency, didn't bother to go back and pick it up.

"Stonehead!" he hissed as he shoved aside a startled lookout and grabbed the man's javelin. With Padmar at his side, he moved to the front of the parapet and launched into a long and raucous attempt at a laugh. The ruse, though hideously unconvincing, gave him time to assess the situation. The Soterion guards had deserted their posts and were lined up with a good-looking stranger holding a long spear. And there, standing next to him... Oh yes! It was her alright, older but still striking. Roxanne, his obsession, his beautiful Nemesis.

Her presence kindled in him a dreadful fire. The flames of failure teased, tormented, and finally consumed him. The pain surpassed the Z-branding of his childhood, swallowing up all other thoughts and desires. Reason fled. In that blind instant, one action alone could assuage his pain: he must kill that woman!

And so it was that Timur the Terrible raised his javelin and cast it at Roxanne. And so it was, too, that Navid the Defender – the noble, loyal Navid – sacrificed his life by throwing himself into its path. The steel point passed clean through his ribs and pierced his heart.

Cyrus' oldest and dearest companion was dead before he hit the ground. The terrible stillness that descended over the scene was eventually broken by a melancholy howl. On and on it went, echoing off the walls, into the trees and across the mountains like the wailing of a legendary host at the loss of its leader. With one soulless exception, all who heard it, even those far away in the square and working on the terraces, shivered with pity for poor, bereaved Corby.

Falling to his knees, Cyrus cradled his dead comrade in his arms. There were no words for his sorrow. Beside him, Sammy began to cry. Roxanne stood open mouthed, looking first at the corpse at her feet, then at the devil on the wall.

Unintentionally, Padmar gave Timur the excuse he needed. "What have you done, Abhay?" she asked quietly as Corby's unhappy wail died down.

"Done?" he retorted. Having wrestled his feelings back under control, he saw that maybe all was not lost. He turned to the warriors around him. "So perish all traitors!" he cried. "It's

223

as I told you, isn't it? That idiot Yash got the wrong woman, but we have now found the right one – and there she is, still with the false Constants who have come to cheat us of what is ours.

"Snake-tongued, aren't they? See how they have tricked our own guards into joining them, just as they tricked Yash's patrol."

Padmar hesitated for a moment. Her doubts about Abhay would have to wait. Once more the situation required command and authority. Abhay had shown such qualities, albeit rather crudely, and she had to do the same. She was, after all, the acting Emir of Alba.

"Abhay is right!" she shouted. "We will allow no traitors beyond our walls, Constant or not."

She pointed at Roxanne. "Except you. You are welcome. You have returned from Yonne to help us, so please enter. Guards, allow in the Z-marked woman and shoot dead anyone who tries to accompany her!"

The Alban warriors heard her words in silence. They might not like what they had heard, but an Emir, acting or otherwise, had to be obeyed. Lacking Yash's strength, independence and iron sense of justice, they would do as their commander had ordered, opening the gates to one stamped as an enemy and shutting them against former colleagues and their friends.

Roxanne knew there could be no discussion. If she so much as hinted to Cyrus what she was going to do, he would stop her. Time was short and Timur's violence made it plain that Taja's plan had failed. The key was inside the walls of Alba and she alone was allowed in.

Lost in his thoughts as he gazed at Navid's lifeless face,

Cyrus hardly heard Roxanne whisper as she hurried past. "I'll be fine, Cy. And whatever you do, don't try to follow me."

What was that? Who'll be fine? He looked up. The gate opened wide enough to admit a single person… "No! Roxanne, no! Come back!"

Before he had time to lay down the body of his friend and scramble to his feet, the gate had closed. He had not even said goodbye. Corby turned from the corpse of his master and started licking Cyrus' hand. Seeing his friend's distress, Sammy clung tenderly to his arm. "It's alright, Cyrus," he said between sobs. "Your Roxanne knows what she's doing, don't she? Trust her!"

At that moment, Cyrus did not feel like trusting anyone. Here he was, far from a home he had abandoned, accompanied by only a broken-hearted dog and a weeping boy. Zavar was dead; Navid was dead; goodness knows what had happened to Taja; and now his dearest Roxanne had entrusted herself once more to the monster who had twice sought to destroy her life. It was all too dreadful, too depressing to contemplate. It was finished.

On the other side of the wall, a peculiar procession had formed. At its head marched Timur, Roxanne on his left, Padmar on his right. My two women, he smirked; and if I had to choose between them, the short, squat one wouldn't stand a chance. He was bored with her already and looking forward to getting to work on Roxanne.

Behind Timur there followed several dozen marching Defenders. As the column made its way towards the square, word spread quickly about events by the gate, and small crowds of Albans turned out to cheer the returning hero. He'd done it! That strange-looking man had actually found the literate woman from Yonne who would open the Soterion and read the secrets of the Long Dead! Excited by the noise, young children ran out of the houses and danced along, whooping and clapping, in front of the parade.

Timur had triumphed.

As the party entered the square, the atmosphere changed. There were plenty of people waiting, mostly archers, but none of them was cheering or waving. Yash and his patrol were still standing beside the well, as Padmar had ordered. At their feet, laid out on the cold stone, was something Timur recognised at once. He had seen so many – indeed, he had seen this particular one before. It was a naked corpse, the horribly, brutally mutilated corpse of Taja, sometime Mudir of the West Tower.

"Abhay," cried Yash when the procession was ten paces from him, "did you do this?"

Letting go of Padmar's hand while maintaining his tight hold on Roxanne, Timur took a couple of steps forward. "Let me see…Yes, I believe I slew this traitor. She deceived us."

"Liar!" shouted Yash. "It is you who have deceived us. She was a good, honest Constant who gave up her life so Roxanne might live."

Padmar made one last effort to maintain her authority and dispel her gathering cloud of doubt. She turned to the Defenders who had accompanied her and ordered Yash's immediate arrest. At a signal from Yash, the archers in the square raised their loaded bows.

Yash advanced to the edge of the well. "Albans!" he cried. "After all those winters of peace and harmony, are we going to start killing each other now? Of course not! There is only one person whom everyone – including Abhay – trusts to tell the truth. Roxanne, you know what's happening. Tell us!" He pointed at Timur. "Who is this man?"

Roxanne, her arm held fast by the man she detested, edged nearer to the well. "My name is indeed Roxanne," she began. "I am a Constant from the community of Yonne. Long ago, we were approached by a deputation from this community with a request for assistance. You had found what you believed was the Soterion…"

As she spoke, Roxanne's mind went back to the occasion of a similar speech in front of Emir Leiss and the Majlis of Della Tallis. She had just met Cyrus then, the man who had believed in her from the outset. It was his unfailing faith, support and love that had kept her going – Oh, how she wished he were here now to give her strength!

"We agreed to help you," she continued, "but our mission was ambushed and destroyed by the Grozny Zeds, the foulest of all the barbarian hoards. I was the sole survivor. As a prisoner, I saw how the tribe's unique and malevolent strength depended on its fiendish leader. Alone among the Zeds, he combined pitiless cruelty with a frightening intelligence."

Roxanne fought to ignore the growing pain of Timur's claw-like grip. "To save my life that I might one day escape and continue my mission to the Soterion," she went on, "I told my captor about the existence of the cave. He pursued me here after my escape, wheedled his way into your confidence, tricked you and lied to you."

The whole square stood motionless as the ghastly truth dawned. "Men and women of Alba, there is no such person as Abhay, the lost Constant." She pointed to Taja's mutilated corpse. "Would a Constant have done that? Would a Constant have tried to kill me, as he did by the wall? You know the answer, don't you?

"This monster standing beside me, who clings to you like a poisonous parasite, is in fact Timur, Malik of the Grozny Zeds!"

As the words of revelation and denunciation died away, the angry crowd instinctively surged forward. For an instant, Roxanne thought Timur's only interest was in saving himself. But he let go of her arm only to draw a small dagger from his belt. As he thrust it into her chest, their eyes met for one last time. Green on red, kindness on cruelty, good on evil. Although dizzy with the pain spreading through her like venom, she held his awful gaze until he looked away, defeated.

From the mouths of Yash and Roxanne and in the body of poor Taja, the Albans had all the evidence they needed of Timur's guilt. It was left to the archers of Alba to administer the penalty.

The condemned man had run no more than three paces before the commands "Take aim! Shoot!" rang out across the square. Fifty arrows whirred like hornets through the morning air and buried themselves in their target. Timur the Terrible stood transfixed for a moment – a hideous pincushion parody of a Long Dead martyr – then sank silently to the ground. Unmoving, he lay like a slaughtered porcupine in the spreading pool of his blood.

Roxanne's wound, though serious, was not immediately fatal. While some of the onlookers rushed to her aid, others seized the broken Padmar and led her away to prison. Yash and Jannat, having checked that Roxanne was in no immediate danger, hurried to tell Cyrus and Sammy what had happened.

On Yash's command, the gates of Alba were opened wide to welcome in the rest of Roxanne's party. The Soterion guards held back to let the visitors enter first. Through the shadow of the archway, the remaining members of the mission passed together: a large, sorrowful-looking dog at the heels of a pale-faced man with a tear-streaked face who held tightly to the hand of a young, half-blind boy.

Willing hands carried Roxanne to a nearby house where she was laid on a bed and made as comfortable as her condition allowed. Cyrus was soon at her side, holding her hand and whispering to her during her moments of consciousness. Outside, Yash supervised the lifting of the lion. When it had been placed on the ground next to the plinth, he examined the place where it had rested. There was nothing there but a smooth surface of stone, lighter in colour where the base of the statue had protected it from the elements. It contained no hollow that might have concealed a key.

Asal hurried inside to speak to Cyrus. "Where exactly did it say the key was, Cyrus?" he asked quietly.

"Beneath the statue."

"Well, we've moved the lion and there's no key underneath, just the stone base."

Cyrus thought for a moment. "Have you looked at the bottom of the statue itself? Under the lion's feet?"

Asal shook his head. "No! Of course! Thank you!" The guard turned to go.

"Asal?"

"Yes?"

"Let me know when you've found it, please. There's someone here to whom it's rather important."

"I will do, Cyrus. Back soon, I hope."

As Asal left the room, Roxanne opened her eyes and smiled at Cyrus. "You're right, Cy. It is rather important. Thank you."

They did not have to wait long. Shortly after a loud cheer arose from the crowd in the square, a small deputation entered the room. First were Yash and Jannat, followed by Asal. Sammy, with Corby at his heels, came last, bearing a small box. On reaching Cyrus, he opened it to reveal a shiny brass key, as clean and bright as on the day it had been made.

Cyrus lifted out the key and held it out for Roxanne to see. "There's writing on it, Cy. My eyes are blurred. Would you read it for me?"

"There's only one word, Roxy. SOTERION. Our mission is over."

She shook her head gently on the pillow. "No, Cy. My part is almost over, but yours hasn't even started yet."

Cyrus struggled to speak. "Without you, Roxy!" he choked.

"I really don't think I could…"

"You must, Cy. My task is done: I have taught you all I know. For my sake and for the sake of everyone, you must go on."

Cyrus' mouth was trembling too much to reply.

At Roxanne's request, that afternoon she was carried on her bed to the Soterion. Cyrus walked beside her, urging her to stay with them and witness the final fulfilment of her mission.

The bed was placed at the mouth of the cave. Alone, Cyrus walked forward and unlocked the door. It swung open easily, letting forth a magical smell of leather and paper and ink and glue such as he had never previously encountered. The new and alluring scent of books was almost irresistible. So, too, was the prospect of having print to read after days and days of learning from scratchings on stones. Nevertheless, he did not enter. He returned instead to the small crowd, stooped down and picked up Roxanne in his arms.

Asking Sammy and Yash to follow with burning brands to give them light, he crossed the threshold of the Soterion like a groom with his new bride. The room was set out as if they were expected. Next to a low couch, where Cyrus gently laid his dying partner, stood a wooden desk and chair. Beyond, covering three walls and rising from floor to ceiling, were shelves and shelves of books.

The light bearers waited respectfully near the entrance as Roxanne, with a supreme effort of will, raised herself on one elbow and looked about her. "Oh, Cyrus!" she gasped. "How I have dreamed of this moment! And now it is here, it is even more wonderful than I had expected. Thank you! Oh, thank you!"

Exhausted, she sank back onto the couch. Cyrus walked over to her and kissed her gently on the brow. "Lie quietly, my Roxy darling," he said softly, "and I will read you to sleep. A bedtime story."

Taking a light from Yash, he searched quickly along the shelves until he found what he was looking for. He returned to the desk and sat down, opening the book before him at the first page. All was still.

"I think you'll like this one, Roxy," he said, turning to see if she was asleep yet. Her eyes were closed and in the flickering light he thought he saw not only Roxanne, but Zavar, Navid and Taja standing there, all smiling down at her. And as he gazed, Roxanne, young again and happy, appeared to rise up and stand beside them.

Cyrus turned back to the book and began to read. "All children, except one, grow up..."

About the author

Prizewinning author Stewart Ross taught at all levels in the UK, the USA, the Middle East and Sri Lanka before becoming a full-time writer. He has published many works, including novels for adults and for children. He has also written plays, lyrics and poetry, and his books have been translated into several languages. As a change from the large garden hut in which he works, Stewart ventures forth to schools, colleges and universities in the UK, France and elsewhere to talk about writing and pass on his passion for words.

For more exciting books from
brilliant authors, follow the fox!
www.curious-fox.com